NAL

DA SAID

NAL

Turtle Point Press, New York

DA SAID

Stuart David

First published by I.M.P. Fiction, London, in 1999

LCCN 2002108628   ISBN 1-885586-71-x

Design and composition by Jeff Clark and Megan Geer
at Wilsted & Taylor Publishing Services

DA SAID

I've begun to think now that I maybe just panicked this afternoon, and then over-reacted some. But I'm still not sure yet, I still don't know for sure.

I am still shaking although, and what I'd really like to be able to do tonight is talk to Nalda. Even just for a little while. To see what kind of words she would have to say.

When I was a boy, you see, I heard Nalda's words nearly all the time; while we sat out on the old sofa in the evenings, or while we swept up leaves in the winter lady's garden through the day. And always she would tell me all about myself and how I'd come to be in her charge, and about the world too, and how things in it worked. And whenever I was confused by something I could go and ask her some questions, and listen to her talk, and slowly things would come back towards sense.

But all of that was a long time ago now. All before the shouting, and all before the people came and Nalda went off. And ever since then I've only been mostly afraid and confused, by the whole of the world and most things inside it. Almost all the time.

And so . . . I still can't tell about this afternoon yet. I still don't know for sure. It's important, because of what lies within my charge, that I live always on my guard. And so lots of times I've misjudged things and over-reacted. But I'm not sure if that's how things were today, and I wonder if Nalda would talk until I could see some other sense in what happened, and it no longer scared me. Or if she would only look at her nail and say, "You did the right thing today. You did the right thing, T . . ."

Ooops. But I almost told you my name there, and I don't mean to do that. Not just yet. Just in case. Just in case of things.

So what I'll do instead, right now, is I'll tell you all about what happened this afternoon, and about why I'm still shaking.

The first thing you need to know, I think, is that for quite a while now I've been working in the gardens of a city park. I suppose that's the first thing. I mostly always try to find work in places like that—first of all because gardening is just about the only thing I know anything about, the only thing that you can use for a job at least. And, secondly, because you never have to be around any other people too much of the time.

In this place, because it was so big, I hardly ever had to talk to any of the other people who worked there at all. There were so many different things to be done most days that, between picking up my tools and getting my orders in the mornings and returning my things to the sheds again in the evenings, I might not see anyone else who worked there all day long. And that's the best way for me. I've never been around other people much, and because of that their ways mostly just get me confused, and then I get nervous.

Anyway, today.

I spent most of it with the grass machine, cutting lawns at the very heart of the gardens. Then, towards finishing up time, I trundled it back to the sheds and got to work wiping the blades clean in there.

I always liked it in the sheds at the end of the day, if there was no one else in there. Most times I tried to work on later than everyone else, so's as they would all be gone by the time I got back. And often, when I had cleaned up my tools and put everything away into its place, I liked to sit beside one of the windows and just be glad that I was finished with gardening for another whole night. And quietly make a wish that I would be freed before the next day from ever having to do it again.

Today although, while I was still wiping the blades clean of grass, I heard the door opening behind me and I grew quite angry that someone had come in to spoil my peace.

2

"Well, that's another one endured and conquered," the voice said, and I knew straight away who it was. I knew at once it was the boy with the pictures on his arms.

"How was yours?" he asked me while he clattered his tools down onto the floor, and I felt myself grow tight and shy. And I fixed my eyes very hard on the blades of the grass cutting machine as I wiped them, even although all of the grass was gone by then.

No one else who worked at those gardens even tried to talk to me after the first one time or two times. I think some of them worked out that it wasn't one of the things I was good at, and that I just didn't know how to do it properly. And some of the others, they became a bit offended by me not ever answering them properly, I think. Either way, they all soon came around to leaving me alone, which was good because it meant I couldn't let any information slip which might put me in danger from them.

But the boy with the pictures on his arms, he was different. He just kept on by talking to me whether I gave him any proper answers or not. It didn't even seem to matter to him very much if I answered at all. And when he had hung up all his spades and things, he dragged the chair from the window across to where I was wiping the blades, and he sat down on it there. Kind of backwards.

"That looks as if you've got them cleaned now," he said to me, while he shifted around on his seat some. But I continued to wipe for a bit more anyway. Then, when I felt like it was getting to be stupid, I got up, all unsure of my movements because I felt like he was spying on me some, and I put the cloth away in a drawer. I even pretended to look for something else in there too, in the hope that he would just go away before I was finished. But he didn't go. He just kept on by sitting there.

When I turned around, although, I noticed he wasn't spying at me at all. He was just touching the pictures on his arms instead, with his fingers, and looking at them all carefully. So seeing my chance I said, "Good night," in a voice that came out all cracked and quiet, and then I hurried out of the shed and closed the door behind me. I even

3

thought I was going to get away with it too, because the door stayed shut until I was quite some steps away. But it was never so easy to escape from the boy with the pictures on his arms, and soon I heard the door opening again and him shouting out to me, while he snapped the padlock of the shed onto the door to lock it up.

"Hang on there," he said as he ran after me. And without even making my eyes look at him I watched him tying a scarf around his head, just from my corners.

"Are you busy right now?" he asked me, while he tightened the knot at the back of his head. "I know you don't speak much, but there's something I want to show you. Something I found today. Are you doing anything else just now?"

I was still thinking of a way to run off from him at that time, and when we reached the end of the track which leads from the sheds to the main path I just turned my back on him quickly, and started walking off.

But he ran after me again.

"It's this way," he said, catching me lightly by the arm. "It's not that way, it's this way." And as we stood looking at each other, and I watched him tugging on the knot behind his head, I suddenly had the idea that maybe he was just lonely for some company, and that was something I knew a bit about.

"It's just something I thought you might like to see," he said. "Something I found in a flower-bed this morning. I'm not quite sure what I'm going to do with it yet, but I know I can trust you not to tell anyone else here anything about it, so you can see it if you want."

He tipped his head to the side then and I was still anxious not to be there, but slowly I turned to face the other way, and he nodded at me.

"You're quite a strange guy," he said. "I hope you don't mind me saying that. But Christ . . . I mean, I'll bet you don't make many friends acting like you act."

Then he laughed and I tried to do a smile to him, but I'm not good at smiling to people. In front of a mirror I can do one alright. When I can

4

watch my own face. But whenever I try to do a smile to someone else I always think it isn't going to work, and then it doesn't work. I kind of make it not, I think, by thinking that. So I looked away towards the flower-beds as soon as I felt it failing, and then I covered my mouth with my hand.

We walked quite a way back through the gardens, the boy with the pictures on his arms and me. And then we walked beyond the gardens and on into the rest of the park. All the way he kept on by talking, the boy, and mostly I didn't even know what he was saying about, like I never do. But he did say a few things about how he wished he didn't have to work in the gardens, and how much he didn't like it, and that surprised me some. It surprised me because I'd always thought it must only be me who didn't like it, and it was a secret I was scared about in case anyone found out and then told me I couldn't work there anymore. And I would be left without my money. So it made me feel good, just that. And I wanted to say something to him about it and agree some. But just when I was getting ready to, he stopped walking, at last, and he pointed over towards a tree near the fence.

"I've hidden it there," he said. "In a hole in the trunk." And he hurried off across the grass and had me follow him.

It was a very broad and old tree which he brought us to, with gnarled and old branches, and a hole at the bottom of the trunk just like he'd said. And while he knelt down in the grass, I leaned against the trunk, and watched him feeling with his hand inside.

"I think you're going to like this," he said to me. "I really do."

And it was just then, as he drew his hand out from in the hole, that all of everything started happening at once.

The thing was, you see, it was a knife he pulled out from in there. A knife with a black, black handle and a long curved blade. And while he stood up again he did the strangest grin to me, and the time started to move very strangely. It went all slow to begin with, and in just a single second I studied the boy's mad grin and some of the pictures on his arms, as well as thinking that what I'd been terrified of for years was very probably just about to happen. Then, as the boy took another step towards me, I watched the sunlight glinting upon his blade. And when he turned it, and the light flashed directly into my eyes, suddenly time was racing instead, moving at twice its normal speed.

And then so was I. Running off towards the fence with my coat flapping on my knees, and my heart thumping terribly.

I heard the boy shouting something behind me, but I didn't hear about what it was, and I didn't turn around any too. I just climbed over the fence as soon as I came to it, ripping my trousers and cutting my leg. And on the other side I tripped on something and fell out full. But I didn't even lie for a minute. I was back up again and running as quickly as I could be. Running and running.

To begin with, I ran back to the room where I'd been staying all the time I was in that city. But as soon as I arrived there I realised about how stupid a thing that was to do. And so as quickly as I could, I put a few important things into a bag and I ran out again.

And all I did do was keep on running then.

Running and running. On and again. For a very long time.

2

Nalda said I first came to her in a complicated array of rags, silent and afraid, when I was just newly two years old. I was wearing a shirt and trousers which had been all tacked up the back with pins, she said, to pull them in tight against my body. And, also, they were all rolled and folded at their tops and bottoms, so that the bits of me which were supposed to stick out still stuck out.

Sometimes when Nalda told me the story about myself she said I came to her in spring, when the flowers were all just coming back to life again. And other times she said I came to her in winter, along a street all covered with a soft blanket of snow. But, no matter what, I was always brought by one of my father's closest companions, in the passenger seat of a very expensive car. And when Nalda had told me about that part she would always make me do a giggle by saying, "And I looked down at this tattered bundle of rags he had handed to me, and I thought to myself . . . 'Good God, I've been cursed! What did I do to deserve this?' "

And she always laughed then too, and pulled me in towards her—in towards all of her dark scarves and skirts, and her warm hair and her chains. And she would rattle me about like that to keep me laughing, until I asked her to tell me about myself more again.

There were so many stories Nalda knew. And I would ask her for the same ones about myself and about things in the world over and again. And whenever I asked her for a new one she would always have a new one too, and after hearing it two times, about, I would have a name for that one also, and I would begin to ask for it over and again too.

But my favourite story was always the one about how I first came to

Nalda in a complicated array of rags, silent and afraid, when I was just newly two years old. That was the one I asked for the most often of all. And after Nalda had rattled me, and I had laughed until I was tired, sometimes she would open the tin she kept in the drawer—if she was in a very special mood. And she would take out what she said were the pins that had been used to tack up my trousers and my shirt that time. And she would let me look at them some.

Even now I still have those pins with me. I keep them in a tin of my own now. And when I grabbed a few things to take away with me this evening the tin was amongst them. It was one of the first things I threw down into my bag.

I wouldn't have left that behind.

I realised, when I had no more breath left for running this evening, that I didn't even have any idea about where I was running to. And so that was why I stopped. What I saw when I did stop, although, was that I was just close by to the bus station. So that was where I went to then.

At first I was going to look at the map outside of the ticket office, to choose a place from there which wasn't too near and wasn't too far away. Somewhere that wouldn't be too easy a place to guess about, or that wouldn't be an obvious place for me to be heading to, just in case the boy would still try to follow me.

But then I had a better idea that I would just go and look at which coaches had the least people inside, and which ones didn't have anyone on who could possibly be the boy with the pictures on his arms, in disguise. And that way, too, it meant that if he should catch up to me soon he couldn't ask at the ticket office about where I had bought my ticket for, and then he would be stuck. If I had just bought my ticket on board.

So I found a coach with hardly any people inside of it at all, which was also going quite a distance away. And I got up on board and settled down towards the back, close by to the door made for emergencies.

Just in case.

It was only a few minutes till the bus left, after I'd got on. But all the time I lay away down low on my seat anyway, hiding where I couldn't be seen from the outside. And all the way out through the city I did the same, just peeking up over the bottom of the window's edge every now and again, to see what I could see. I stayed like that, too, while all of the buildings were getting less, all the way out until it was only fields that were left on both sides of the road, and the city was far away and behind us. And only then, very slowly, did I begin to raise myself up in the seat at last, feeling a little bit safer. And feeling grateful, too, through my shaking, that I had gained some more time to await the thing which I await.

It wasn't until the bus had been going on for over an hour, although, that I first began to wonder if I hadn't maybe just panicked some back in the park before. And then over-reacted.

Before that there hadn't been any doubts in my thoughts at all. I was absolutely sure about what I thought had almost happened. But while I'd been sitting watching the sky getting darker above the fields, with my cloth bag pressed away in tight against my chest, I'd slowly began to wonder just how the boy with the pictures on his arms could possibly have known about me. I hadn't never hardly even spoken to him during all the times he'd tried to speak to me, so I was certain that I'd never let anything slip to him that I shouldn't have. And then, too, as the bus kept moving, I also began to remember about a few kindnesses he had shown to me in the past, and there was one in particular which I kept on by thinking of which really made me think he wasn't that kind of a one at all, and which made me think that maybe the knife really had been something he'd just found and wanted to show me. To try and

9

even make a friend of me. And so that was when I first began to think that perhaps I had just panicked.

Again.

It wasn't long after I'd first arrived in that city, and before I'd been working in those gardens for very long at all, that the boy with the pictures on his arms did the kindness for me that I kept thinking of while the bus rolled.

To begin with, I'd worked mostly in the rose gardens there, over where the gardens joined onto the main part of the park, where lots of young people always came to kick footballs around, or to throw those things like disks to each other.

So the thing that happened was, there was one group of older children who never did used to kick any football around, or throw any disk or anything much at all. Always they just used to drift about mostly, and maybe smoke some cigarettes, and maybe push each other around sometimes. And spit and stuff. So, one day they were all quite close to where I was working, and a few were looking at me, and then one of them shouted out a name at me. I don't remember what name now, but I became quite tight and quite shy. And I got quite awkward about what I was doing and I even blushed some, though I don't know if they could see that. But I didn't shout anything back to them although. And I think that was what turned out to be the wrong thing.

They all came kind of closer then, and they started to all shout the name at me, and then all different things. And I just concentrated hard upon a rose, and pretended to work very absorbed until they went away.

But after that, they kept on by coming back a few days more, and I would get nervous and things as soon as I saw them. And they always stopped to shout for a while. Sometimes they even came closer, and maybe flicked my sleeve or something, or flicked my hair. But always I pretended just to be absorbed by my work, while all of them giggled and shouted, or just made a strange noise. And then one of them curled a fist around the head of a rose once, and said, "What would happen if I pulled this, mister? What would? Would it bleed?"

But still I kept on by staring at what I was doing, and then another one tugged at my sleeve and said, "What would happen if he did that, mister? Would it bleed?"

Then another one, a girl, she said, "Don't you think I look like a rose, mister?" to a lot of shouting and laughing. "I do though," she insisted. "Don't I, mister?"

And she touched my cheek with her fingers, and all of them laughed.

"Would you fuck her, mister?" a boy asked then. "Would you want to?"

And then another girl.

"He would too! Look at him blush . . ."

I still kept on just by seeming like I was absorbed in my work although. Not looking. Mostly I didn't even know what they were saying about, and younger people always make me even more confused than older ones, some of them. So I had no idea at all about what to do.

But that was when the boy with the pictures on his arms came along. Just then. And he grabbed one of them by the arm and he shouted some. And I looked up just quickly and I saw that they all looked pretty scared. Very scared really. And the boy said about what he would do to them if they came around that part again, and he said to them about how I would let him know if they worried me ever any time again, and about how he would get them all one by one if I said that.

One at a time.

I tried to do him a smile just then, but I think it failed quite a lot, and I heard one of the children start to laugh. But the boy with the pictures shouted pretty loudly at him, and he stopped right then, and no one else laughed.

Then, in time, he let go of the one he had grabbed, and they all ran away together then. And I never did see them again.

•

So it was thinking all over that, which really got me to thinking that I'd maybe just panicked today, along with, of course, wondering about how he could possibly have known about me, in the first place.

What Nalda used to say, you see—about people, I mean—was that all but the very few would rip and tear at even the most precious of things to get to that part which would bring them profit and gain. And not just nasty people, she said. But just about all of everyone, almost every person you could ever meet, all except for the very most gentle and kind, and also the most very pure. It wasn't really that they were bad, she said most times, but only really that they were lazy and tired. Or else ignorant of any other way. But whichever, that's what makes up the main reason of why I must keep a distance really, and be careful never to get so close as to let anything slip which could put me into danger from their ways.

But the thing is although, the main thing, I got to wondering for a while on the bus if the boy with the pictures on his arms maybe might even have been just one of the very few that she sometimes said of. Just because of the kindnesses he had shown to me sometimes. And that made me a bit upset in case he had just been trying to make a friend from me, because one of the things I would very much like to have is a friend. And mostly I sometimes think that a girl for a friend would be best. But still . . .

And that made me wish a bit that I could go back, even although I couldn't.

Just in case.

When the bus finally got to where it was going tonight, I waited until all the other people inside had got off and wandered away, before I got down too. Then, with my bag still pressed in tight against my chest, I looked around at where I had got to, and then I looked around for a place to stay for tonight.

I continued being a bit cautious outside to begin with, looking a few times behind me while I walked, despite all of what I'd thought on the bus. Just to make sure that the boy hadn't followed me there. But I soon got to be convinced it was alright, and I soon found a hotel place that looked okay, so I came inside.

Always, in the pocket of whatever shirt I'm wearing, I keep a supply of emergency money ready. Just enough to take me away from wherever I am, on a bus or a train, and to pay for a room for the night wherever I end up, in case something should happen which makes me have to leave. Like it always does.

The room I'm in now looks almost exactly like all the other rooms I've stayed in at times like this. And once I'd been shown in, and I'd locked the door up behind me, I did what I always do first, after up and running. I unfastened my cloth bag and sat down on the bed with it, to see what things I'd brought with me, and what things I'd left behind.

I had the tin with my pins inside, of course. And most of my clothes too, which aren't really many anyway. Then, besides that, I had my can and my utensils, the book with some pages pasted inside that I've saved from newspapers, a couple of special things to eat, and that was all. I'd left a lot behind again, like I always do. I'd left a lot of trinklets and ornaments I'd collected, and some photograph pictures I liked to have on my wall. But what was most important of all was I'd left my jeweller's eyeglass behind, and that will make things a lot more difficult for me.

I found that, one day, just when I was digging up a flower-bed in a park, and I didn't even know what it was at first. But once I'd worked it out, and cleaned it up, I was very pleased at my find. And I started using it the very next morning.

I've been using it every day too, from then. And I even know exactly where I've left it. I can picture it sitting exactly on my bed, back in my last room.

And I could even kick myself.

Usually I always left that lying with my utensils together, but this morning I just brought that through by accident, and laid it down there.

I suppose that's what happens when you leave in a hurry. You sometimes always leave something behind that you'd rather not have forgotten. The trinklets and the photograph pictures don't bother me really so much, but . . .

Curses.

I'll have to buy an old kind of stupid magnifying glass tomorrow again now.

Anyway, although. It feels like as if it's been a long day today. My terror in the park even seems like it could have been a week. And leaving my other room this morning, to walk through the people to the gardens, that seems like it could have been a year.

So what I'm going to do now, I'm going to wash. And then I'll get my can set up, just so's as it's ready. And after I eat some stuff, I'm going to lie down in my bed. And hopefully I'm going to go to sleep.

3

*J*do wonder sometimes, just to myself, what Nalda would think to see me here in places like this. To see some of the cities I've stayed in on my own now, and to see some of the rooms I've stayed in there. Especially the ones inside hotels, that I've spent a few nights in each time after running.

Let me tell you about where Nalda and I used to stay, when I was with her.

I remember that sometimes Nalda used to say some things and some stories about a house where she had once lived in, a time before I first came to her. But mostly she only told about that on days when she had decided to be unhappy about the little caravan we lived in together, and so I didn't like to hear about it, because of how I didn't like her not to like our kind.

In the town where we were, there was an unpaved road running down a hill at the outside edge of the place. And down one side of the road had a long row of white houses, and down the other it had a field which had some things in. It had a tractor which didn't ever move, and sometimes it had some animals, and it had a big rusted water tank or something.

Then, at the very bottom of that road there was a piece of grass, and that was where we stayed. In that caravan.

It was very small. But outside, on the grass, we had an old sofa. And lots we sat out there, when it was warm and when it had dried out after rain. And also, on that piece of grass, there were two trees which Nalda tied a rope on, and on there we hanged our clothes. When they needed to dry.

I liked our caravan, I liked it all the time. But the thing was, it kind of sat in a ditch at one end on that piece of grass, which meant it didn't quite sit straight. And inside the floor sloped a little bit. And that was what sometimes got Nalda to being unhappy, just that.

Mostly she liked it always too, and she always made stories about it, and about how it sloped. But just sometimes it would get her to being unhappy, and I couldn't make her laugh any then. And she would tell instead about that house I said of, and sometimes she would even say about how I was part of the same curse that had made her not be there. Having to look after me was part of the same bad spell. And she would hate our van then.

So I do wonder sometimes what she would think, to see some of the cities I've seen. And to see how nice some of the rooms are that I've stayed in.

There.

I went out again here as soon as I was ready this morning, and the very first thing I did was look around at what gardens are here, both public and private ones. Then, once I had did that, I started to ask around about work at the places I'd seen.

It might amaze you, like it sometimes amazes me, about how easy I find it to talk to people when I'm asking after work, compared to how stupid and hopeless I am around people at any other time. And how afraid and uncertain I am of them. But it's not quite so strange really. And mostly it has to do with a kind of spell Nalda did when I was very, very young, and which still works now.

From about the first time when I can remember, you see, I was always at work with Nalda—because of how I was in her charge, and she couldn't leave me back at home by my own. So I was always with her when she went to look for work too, whenever we had finished off in one garden for a while and had to have something new.

So, how it was, because I was always there with Nalda and I already helped her to do all most of the work, she also began to try and get me to help do some of the asking too, when I was still quite young. She said, then, that eventually a day would come when I would have to do it all for myself, and that it was important to learn. And that was for why she tried to get me started.

I can remember clear now the first time she tried to get me to do it, although. And I can still remember clear too my tears, and the feeling which made it much easier to refuse Nalda and to fight against her, rather than to approach those frightening gates, and those doors. And all of the men and ladies behind.

"But it's only a few words," Nalda kept on by saying at all of those times. "Just: Do you need any work done in your garden? Only that. That's all. People will be much kinder when it's a pretty little boy that's asking, T . . ." (Ooops, I almost said it again there.) "And then we'll get more extra work, and we can have those especial cakes again."

But each time I stamped and stamped, and she had to do it herself, all until the time when she made my spell.

The way it worked was, she put it on me very gradually. Instead of ever having to just go up and ask the whole thing, like she had always tried to make me, it was like we would both go to the door together. And the first time I would say "Do . . . ," just "Do." And then Nalda would say the rest. And each time I said one word more of the question, which was easy. And at last I said it all, and when I'd said it all once, the spell was on me. And then it was easy. And from then on I was always excited when it got time to look for some new work, because then I could get to do what I could do. And whenever it was, I would almost be a beggar to Nalda to let me do the asking. And I would even go to the gates and the doors by myself, because I had the spell. And it was true what Nalda had said, we really did get more work to do that way.

So that's why I find that one thing all easy and okay. And my spell hasn't never faded. The one thing I've learned that Nalda didn't know, although, is the difference with a city from a town.

17

In the cities, especially when it's with parks or such, the gardens are so big you can work there for a very long time. And that even means you get proper money too. Paid like other people's money is paid. I learned about it in one of the first times I went to a city. When I asked at a house and a lady said "No," but also she told me to try at the park and I did and it worked.

So that's always the first place I try now, at parks, and it was the first place I tried here this morning too. They didn't need anyone although—they had everyone they needed there they said. But that's the other thing about a city too. Mostly if they don't need anything they almost always say about somewhere that might. And the man, today, he said about the hospital, of how he thought they might just need one. And he even drew me a picture of how to get there, and wrote down what buses and things.

The best thing, too, is that I can talk good to people about gardens. I just don't get confused any, because of how I know exactly where I am, and because I don't get scared either that I might let something dangerous about myself slip. And I just forget about all other things and I talk.

So the lady, at the hospital, she said I'd mostly be fine she thought. The amount of money she said it would be for each week was much less than I got in the last place but, the thing is, there are little quarters that come with the job. A little building away down in the gardens, separated from the hospital building, which the lady said was once a garden cottage many old years ago, when the hospital building was still someone's huge house.

"Would they be of any use to you?" she asked me. "Or do you already have a place of your own?"

So I shyly asked to see them, because of how there was something I had to know first. And she took me down and I grew all awkward and uncertain while she was trying to talk to me about other things, and about myself.

The quarters were fine for me although. They were a little building made from red stones, with a kind of peaked roof. And on the inside, although it was a bit dusty and smelled a bit from being closed up a while, it still looked quite nice. And it had one room which had a table and a bed, and a sink by the dusty window. And also a cooking machine too. Then it had a door which went through to a tiny toilet and bath place. So I just nodded to the lady and said in a wobbly voice that it would be fine for me to stay inside of. And then, as soon as I could, I hurried off.

So I start tomorrow morning, and I move in there tomorrow too. I am some worried about how much the lady might talk to me on all of the days, but mostly I'm glad to be sorted out again. And to have somewhere to live, and something to provide me with enough money to live there, while I'm waiting . . .

4

*H*ave I told you any proper things yet about the lady who used to live in our town who didn't like winters? I've been just about to a few times, but I don't think I quite did do any. So, instead, I'll say some here about her now.

She lived on the far away and other side of the town from Nalda and me, the winter lady. And always, when spring had already been making the flowers come back alive again for a few weeks, Nalda would say one day, "I think the winter lady must be back by now, T . . ."

And so, as soon as what job we were doing got to be finished up with, the very first place we tried next would be the winter lady's.

Her house was huge, made up of these very light-brown stones, with lots of ivies and vines clinging to them. And her garden was huge too. It even had a little summer house in it, about just the same size as our caravan. And, sometimes, when Nalda was always unhappy, she would always say, "You can be sure the floor won't slope inside of the winter lady's house. You can be sure of that."

Anyway, although. Hers would always be the first place we tried for new work after the flowers had started. And, most times, she would be already waiting for us, and there was always lots of work to be started and done. Even just in cutting things back and chopping down the grass. And even cleaning up last year's leaves, because of how the winter lady had been gone since before it was even the end of summer.

The thing was, you see, the winter lady only stayed in our own town from after spring had started until just before the end of summer, each year. And, in fact, that was the only part of time she ever stayed anywhere. Because what she did, Nalda said, was to follow the living seasons around the globe.

"Summer is always somewhere," Nalda told me. "It's like the moon." And she explained like when it's winter on one side of the world, then summer is on the very opposite one. And the same with autumns and springs too. Which makes the summer and winter move round a little bit. So the winter lady, she just followed the seasons around which she wanted, and Nalda said she had houses in all places. And all just as big as the one in our own town.

What I always did, whenever she came out to talk to Nalda while we were working there, I used to spy at her very secretively, when she wasn't looking any. And I was always amazed about how much younger than Nalda she looked to be, even although she was so very much older. And it always amazed me too to know that one day I would look older than the winter lady. Because the thing was, you see, the winter lady was more than three hundred years old. Only, on the outside, she had stayed by being the age she was when she last lived through a winter. And Nalda said that was how it happened, if you didn't pass through all of the seasons each year, and didn't share in all the dying and rebirth of all of the plants and the leaves, you wouldn't never grow on any. But too, she said, if ever the winter lady was to live through a winter somewhere now she would age all of those years she'd missed at once, and her body would suddenly become all of the age which she really was.

What finally reminded me to say about all that stuff was coming back here to the hospital again, and getting fixed into my new little quarters. And the reason for why it reminded me is because the grounds and gardens here remind me just a little of the grounds and gardens around the winter lady's house. They're just a little bit the same.

The hospital sits up high and tall here, with broad lawns that tumble down from the back of the building, until it all flattens out at the bottom into the large gardens and lawns, with their hedge-lined pathways and lattice archways and flower-beds. And that's kind of how the winter lady's looked too. Her house sat up high, and her gardens were mostly all behind the building, sloping down to begin with. It was all much smaller I suppose, but her summer house was in just about the same position that my little quarters are—down in a corner near the back wall. With the same kind of peaked roof, and ivy on the walls. So that was all of the things which remembered me to say about her in the end, just because of how this place looks a tiny bit the same.

I arrived here in about the middle of the morning yesterday, after I'd packed up all my things again, being very careful not to leave anything behind this time. The woman who's my employer did talk to me some when I first arrived. She said about how she was glad to have me with them, and then she took a key from a drawer and walked all the way down the lawns with me, and along the path to my quarters, where she unlocked the door.

"Here we are now," she said once we got there. "So, like I said, I'll give you some time to unpack and get settled in. And then I'll send Frank down to show you around the gardens properly, and to explain exactly what your duties involve. I'm sure it will all be well within your capabilities though," she said. "You seem very knowledgeable about the whole thing."

And as she handed me the key I tried to drag in past her, with my bag and things. Before I could get right inside the door, although, she came in just a bit behind me and still stood there. So I put my bag up onto the table I've told you about before and waited for her to go away.

"The only thing I'd ask," she said then, "is if you're playing music or having visitors anytime, if you could keep the noise to a reasonable level after eight o'clock. To avoid disturbing any of the patients." And after that she did a smile and said, "So I'll send Frank down in maybe about half an hour?" And at last she stepped outside of the door and did another smile, and I tried one back.

And the thing was although, for once, it didn't go too badly. I don't suppose it was perfect or like that, but it didn't go so badly as sometimes. And I managed to hold it like that till the woman turned and left. And then I shut the door.

●

I didn't unpack or anything before Frank came down. Once I had locked my door and had a real and proper look around my rooms, I just sat for a while by my little window, looking out at the grounds. But the most surprising thing was that there was none of the dust left on the window like when I'd first seen it before. In fact, there was none of the dust left anywhere, and all of the closed up smell was gone too. So it must have been that the woman had cleaned it out for me, or else had someone else to do it. And I felt like that was very kind of her, and it made me feel quite good.

It was closer to an hour before Frank finally came to the door although, and I had started to get quite nervous by then, just thinking about him. But I was mostly alright once we got started, because it was mostly just the garden he talked about, and my spell helped perfect with that.

He was about the same age as the woman who employed me, Frank. They're both quite old. And Frank has a thick grey beard and a round red face with some more grey hair there on top. And he has a big stomach too. He was kind to me too, although. And at one bit, before he left me at the end, he did me a wink and said to me, "None of the best gardeners we've had here have ever been too keen on talking. So, from the evidence, there's a good chance you should be the very best of all."

Mainly my duties are upkeeping the lawns, and all of the flower-beds and the hedges. But also I have to keep all the paths clean, tend to the pond and the trees, and just generally keep the whole place looking good.

He showed me around in the sheds too while we were out there. And he showed me where all the tools are stored, and the cutting machines too. And he said about how important it was to make sure I always looked after and cleaned them properly. That was the only thing he would be strict for, he said.

"Well, that and the garden being always in beautiful condition," he added and did a laugh. I tried a smile back to him too, but I don't think it was so good that time, although I don't think he was looking at me much anyway.

"Anyway," he said then. "Just take things quite easy today, and get yourself settled in. Maybe do a little, and get to know the garden a bit better, then you can get yourself started properly tomorrow."

And he asked me for the keys for my quarters then, and when I gave them to him he hooked the key for the sheds onto my ring too and gave them back to me. Then, after he'd said that thing I told you about the best gardeners not talking much, he said he would bugger off then and leave me to it.

And he did.

*G*uess what thing I really like about this place; since I have to be here without a choice anyway. My favourite thing is having my own little quarters. That's what I really like. And I didn't ever have anything like that from any time before.

What one of my wishes is, for when all of my waiting has finally paid off, is to have my own big and luxury place to stay. And on all of the times when I've had to live in tiny city rooms, with all kinds of people bumping on the walls around about of me, and when it's always scared me to have so many around that I could be in danger from, that's one of the wishes which always helped me a little bit to endure.

I didn't never dare to wish that I would have such a private little place of my own any time before then. I didn't ever think that could happen. So it's very especial. And it's like a miniature kind of practice for when I do have the place I really want. It lets me have a small idea of how fine things will be then.

It even makes me not hate working here quite so much as I usually do in places, just because of that. Although, not to lie, I still don't like it at all. It still makes my head light to think of how I would feel if it was to be forever. And if it wasn't only short-term and temporary.

It makes me sad sometimes now to think of the boy with the pictures on his arms like that, to think of how he seemed to find it just so hateful and just such a back-breaker as I do. And then to think of how he'll probably have to do it forever, and that he probably even knows it.

To think on it like that I can almost understand why he would try such a thing like he did that time, when I ran off. Just a bit I can. And I can understand why a lot of others might do it too, if they could know about me.

There are people I see sometimes, in cities. Just people sitting on a bench or by the window in a cafe, or maybe sitting on a bus or an underground train; and just by the sadness in the way their body sits, or by the way their faces look, I can see that they aren't where they want to be. But that, also, they've already been there for a very long time, and they're probably going to be there a long time longer, and possibly forever. And if I ever think of myself like that, living like I do so lonely and with so much of this back-break gardening, it can make me weep a little to imagine how it would be to be like those ones are, without any promise that soon the waiting will be over. And without any promise that soon I will have that big and luxury place and then all lots of especial friends, and special clothes too, and be free of what makes me so afraid so often. And, most importantly of all, be free at last of all this having to garden.

So the thing is, when I tell you now about how I want to stay here for just as long as I can, and not panic off again, you'll know that I only mean for as long as it's necessary for me to be waiting. And only as opposed to having to find yet one more place after this one to wait in, where, most probably of all, it would be one more of those tiny city rooms again, rather than my own little quarters. So that's why I'm going to try and stay here until it ends. That's why I'm going to be very careful not to let or make any of the things happen which have got me into running off in the past.

And it's also for why I went straight into working my best on that first day here, rather than resting any at all like Frank had said for me to do. Just so's as how he wouldn't decide to send me off because he thought I was no use, or idle.

What I'd thought I would do, at first, was maybe just tidy the edges of the grass around the flower-beds and things, because I'd noticed of how raggedy they were while Frank was showing me about the place.

But when I went back out again, after unpacking my things and getting my can all set up and ready, I decided to do something a bit more, and I went looking around properly on my own, to see what needed doing most.

The hedges were all needing to be trimmed, and a lot of the climbing flowers on the archways would have gotten Nalda to muttering, because of how unruly they'd been allowed to grow. But the best thing I thought I should try to do was tidy up the pond, across on the other side of the garden from my own little quarters, because of how you could hardly even see the surface of the water anymore.

So once I'd decided I went and unlocked the sheds, to get out what I needed, and then I got on by getting started.

I cut back all the grass growing out into the pond for first off, and then I cleaned out all of the leaves that were lying on the surface, and tidied up some of the water flowers growing there too. It wasn't until I did all that, although, and was getting ready to clear out the rest of the leaves which had all sunk in and deeper down, that I learned there were some fish in there. Orange and pale white ones they are, with long fins that float behind them like scarves. So I was very careful while I was taking the leaves out then. And, once I had, I tidied up the little trees around the pond a bit too. Then I just sat and quietly watched the fish for a little while. Watched them glide and drift, in and out between the stems of the water flowers, until it got me to thinking of this ring which Nalda used to have.

There was a silver ring she used to wear on her smallest finger, you see, and sometimes when we were working she would always have me keep it in the pocket of my jacket for her, in case it fell off and got lost. And the reason for that was because, one time before I ever came to her, she had lost the same ring off a river bridge.

The story about that was one of the ones I asked her for quite often, sometimes when I was giving her the ring back as we were walking home, or sometimes when we sat out on our sofa in the evenings. And

I would move the ring around with my finger when she was holding my hand then, and ask her to say about the fish. And sometimes she would do a laugh and say, "What fish? I don't remember about it."

"Yes you do," I would say back. "You do, Nalda. Tell about it."

And she would always do a laugh again and say, "Remind me, then. I can't seem to remember what you're talking about."

"Yes . . . Remember . . . It fell off into the river, and you saw it going down inside the water. And you cried for one whole year until when one day you bought a fish from the sea and it was there inside. You do, Nalda. And the fish had ate it when it was swept to sea."

Then she would say she remembered, just a bit, and when I told her to say it she would tell me that I just had. But, always then, she would tell it full.

And I would join in at some bits I remembered best.

That was really what happened although, to the silver ring. And she got it back like that, from in a fish. Not an orange or white one although, like the ones here. Just a normal fish for eating.

From the sea.

By the time I was finished with looking at the fish that day it was already about four o'clock in the afternoon, so all I did then was dispose of all of the leaves and grass and lilies I had tidied, and put away all of my tools back into the shed. Then I left the hospital grounds again for a little while, to find a place where I could stock up with some food and things.

It's quite far on from the middle part of the city, my hospital place, but I found some small and quiet shops not so far away, where I finished off almost all that was left in my emergency fund. And then I returned to my little quarters again, where I cooked up a few of the things on the stove. And when they were ready I pulled the table over closer to the window and sat to eat them there, looking out to the trees around the fish pond, and still delighting in suddenly having my own kind of place.

I'll tell you about one thing although, which I always like to do wherever I am. I realised I most probably won't be able to do it here when I went out to get that food, just because of how I'm actually living where I work.

Wherever I've stayed before, you see, I've always had quite a way to walk each day from my city room to wherever I'm working. And like that, in cities, you get used to seeing a lot of the same strangers in the same places at the same time. Every day. So what I've always done before, I've always liked to watch out for a girl or a woman who makes my heart go quiet and loud, who I could always be most times certain I would see in a particular place at a certain time every day, either on my way to working or on my way home.

In that last place I was, it was a girl with black hair in a gold clasp who would always be standing at a bit where buses stopped outside the park, every morning. And I always spied at her face when I was closer, until I could see that she was just about to see me. And then I would look off and around, so's as how she wouldn't get to know.

Then, in the place before that, there was a woman with soft eyes and beautiful arms in the shop where I bought bread. And always I liked to hear her talking to other people while I queued. And then I always got nervous with my money when it was me next to pay.

And I remember, too, there was another park I worked in once where every day, if it was a Thursday, there was this one who would come to the same bench for a short time in the afternoons. And always she would read, and always she would wear a pale blue scarf on her throat, and a woollen dress which was very tight around. But the only thing was, she didn't ever come if it rained. So every day, if it was a Wednesday, I would hope my very best that it would be dry the next day.

It's a thing that always makes me be not so lonely sometimes, doing that. And, always, I put a promise on myself too that when my waiting should end then maybe I could make a friend of whatever person it is at that time. Because I would no longer have a need to be careful, and also because they wouldn't hate my poorness then. But, really, that's something I can't do in this place. And while I was eating those first things it made me a little bit tired to think so.

But now I don't really suppose it matters so much. Not compared to having my own little quarters.

●

I saw Frank wandering down in the gardens that same evening, while I was still sitting by my window for a while, after I'd eaten all of my things. He went over and stood by the pond for a while too, dropping handfuls of stuff into it from a bucket he was holding, and while he looked around at the things I had done to it I watched him all closely, to see if I could tell what he thought about any of it. But I couldn't get to having a proper view of his face. And then, just when I thought I was about to, I saw that his eyes were turning straight towards my window, and I had to duck down and move away, in case he should find out that I was spying from there.

I hoped for a while after that although that he might come around to my door and say if he liked how I was doing things or not. But he didn't come, and when finally I went back to the window, to look at him again, he had gone away and the garden was empty. And I began to worry for in case he didn't like what I'd done at all, and he would decide to send me away.

What I did in the end, after I'd tidied all my dinner things away, was I went back out on my own again to watch at the fish, just in case he would see me standing there and come down to tell me what he thought. But although I stood there for a while he didn't come down.

The pond still looked to me like I had done good although. It still looked much better to me than from before I'd got started. And because I'd done a lot of ponds with fish in before, with Nalda, I knew I hadn't taken out too many of the lilies to make the fish annoyed. So if it was true that Frank didn't like it I didn't know why at all.

I decided the thing was, although, that even if he was going to move me on, he wasn't going to do it before the next day. I could still have my own special quarters for that night. And there was every chance that by the time the next morning came my burden would be lifted forever. And it wouldn't matter by any at all then.

So I gave up waiting for him after that and I went back inside. And for the rest of the night I read the book which I keep all of my clippings pasted into, just to lift myself up some. In spirit.

And to pass the time.

6

*I*t's strange how many different things I've been remembering all
about the winter lady during the last few days, just because of the
little bit this place reminds me of her grounds. Almost every time I go
out into the garden I remember something else it seems. But the thing
is, I remembered something today which has begun to make me worry
quite some, when I think about it along with thinking about the boy
with the pictures on his arms.

I've always thought about it sometimes before, without ever really
forgetting about it any. But it wasn't until I thought of it after what happened with the boy with the pictures that I saw what it maybe might
mean. And it's begun to make me even more fearful than I usually am
of everything and things.

The thing I remembered about, you see, was a time when the winter
lady stayed on just a bit longer in our place than usual. Right up till the
very end of summer it was. And I got this idea then that if she was to
stay for just a few weeks more I would see her start to age in that rapid
way Nalda had always said about.

We were all finished up with working at her place by then, Nalda and
me. But sometimes I would always run up there on my own in the evenings, to spy out for her. And one night, when I was hiding by a bush
watching out for her maybe coming into the garden, I saw three leaves
lying on her lawn. Not just leaves that a strong wind had blown down
although, not healthy summer leaves. They were curled and brown
and dead. And I quickly ran out from my hiding place and picked them
up from the grass, then I stuffed them up inside my shirt and ran home.

I had this idea, just then, that if I could collect every single leaf that fell into the winter lady's garden before she could see it, then, just maybe, autumn would arrive without her knowing. And then I could see her become a truly old woman.

So every morning after that I went up to her garden before Nalda and I went to work, and every evening too after we had finished. And every day there were more leaves to collect, and even no matter how clear I got it in the mornings there would still be just as many to gather up the same evening again.

One night, although,when I was stuffing leaf after leaf into my pockets and into the bag that I took with me by then, the winter lady came out, and she saw me. She crept down quietly so that I didn't even know she was there, not until it was too late I didn't. And when she reached me she took hold of my arm and did a loud laugh.

"What are you doing, T . . ." she asked me, still with her laughing. "Why are you gathering all of those? So's there won't be so many to do when you come again next year?"

I wasn't nearly so nervous and afraid then as I am now, but I still got quite a big fright. And she still had to coax me for a while before I could say anything much at all.

"I was thinking to hide them from you," I said in the end. "So's you wouldn't know it was winter, and then you wouldn't go away."

I didn't say any about how I wanted to see her old although, just that. That was all. And then, while I was spying into her face to see if any of it was beginning to start yet, she said the thing I'm telling about. She pushed some hair over on my head, and bent closer down to me, and then she said, "You know, you have something very special inside . . ."

And I've always wondered of just how she could possibly have known, because Nalda swore on lots of times that both of us, me and Nalda, were the only people in the whole world who knew. She promised always that she never ever would tell anyone else in the whole world, to keep me safe. And that's what's made me worried now, since what happened with the boy with the pictures. Because I've begun to think that maybe there's a way that certain people can just tell. Without me having to let slip on any kind of anything at all. And if that really is true it means I might be in more danger than I ever once thought about before.

Which makes me very afraid.

All the worries I had from before about Frank not liking my work, and about him sending me away because of it, they've all gone now. I kept on by just working on things I knew needed doing for a few more days, and always I kept wishing that Frank would come to say what he thought and always he didn't come. But then, just a few days ago while I was inside the shed getting what tools I needed for the day, the woman who employed me stuck her head in through the door of the sheds. And she asked me if I had a moment or two to spare, to discuss a few things with her about the gardens. It gave me a bit of a fright, the way she appeared. But when I'd got over it I came out into the sun beside her, and while she talked I looked at her hands, and at her chin and things.

"You've been doing a fine job so far," she said to me. "The gardens are already looking twice as good as they did before. And Frank thinks so too . . ."

I was looking at her hands while she said about that, and I got quite surprised about how far the bones on the back of her wrists stuck up, compared to mine. She's quite thin and frail, the woman who employed me. And her hair is a kind of grey and brown colour. And also, too, whenever she talks sometimes she takes out this handkerchief which she keeps tucked up inside of her sleeve, and she cleans her glasses a bit with it.

So she did that, while we were there, and then she began to unfold out this thing in her hands which was kind of like a map. And she held it out for me to see.

"Now," she said, "What we've been thinking about for a while now is having a couple of new flower-beds. Do you think you would be up to that?"

So I nodded some, because I knew I would.

"Alright," she said, and I heard her doing a quiet laugh. "You're very shy, aren't you?" she said. "Why don't you come a little bit closer so's you can see this thing properly?"

But I was feeling kind of stiff and tight, and I was also trying to hide her from seeing whatever it might be that sometimes gives me away. So mostly I just stayed where I was, and leaned my head a bit closer in to her map thing. And she laughed some again.

"Alright, then," she said. "Alright. Just however."

Once she had flattened the map out properly although I could see it okay from there, and she explained to me about what the things on it were, and pointed out the shapes that were to be the new flower-beds.

"I think it's going to be mostly rose-bushes and shrubbery," she said. "But they won't be arriving for a few days yet, so that'll give you some time to get prepared for digging them in."

She handed the map to me after that, and as I looked over it I could feel her spying at me closely.

"Does it seem okay?" she asked me after a moment. "Is it all clear enough?"

And without lifting my eyes up any I nodded, and I thought I could hear her mouth making a smile.

"Okay," she said. "Okay. I'll go and let you get on with it. Is that alright?"

And as soon as I nodded again I heard her footsteps moving away across the grass, and I went back into the sheds to find the different things I would need, instead of the ones I already had.

⬤

So that's what I've spent the last few days by doing, just working on making those new flower-beds. Cutting their shapes on the lawns, turning the soil, digging in some fertilising bits. And then, yesterday, the woman came back down to say that the flowers would all be arriving in the afternoon. So I spent most of that day and most of today working out just how they should be arranged, and then digging them in.

I didn't finish up with the whole thing until early this evening, and by then, to be true, I had gotten to be pretty ill of it all. I was in quite a curious mood too, by then. Resentful and angry, really resentful and angry that I still had to be there doing that, breaking my back, still after so much waiting.

There had been a time, when I was putting the very first of the flowers in yesterday, when I hit this white stone amongst the earth with the very tip of my trowel, and it gave me the most curious feeling. I had been in a bit of a drift at the time, and I wasn't even concentrating so much on where I was, so the first thing was that I thought my moment had come, at last, until I realised I was out there in the garden. But it did lift my spirits high, somehow. And it got me back to realising what everything is about and for, and even to believing that it wouldn't be too long now; surely any day now.

But by the end of today I just was so wearied out by the work that it had all disappeared again, and I was only angry and resentful. And while I was digging in the last few roses, the way I was feeling made me deal with it all a bit too impatiently. And the way I dealt with it made me rip the back of my hand on some of its thorns. And, for a few minutes, that frayed my temper completely.

I threw my trowel down and punched the grass from where I was kneeling. And when I had worn myself out by that I just rolled onto my side and kept on by whispering over and again, "This isn't where . . . It just . . ."

Till eventually I got to be calmer again, and till I got to be a bit less angry, and only tired and worn. Then I went and washed my cut hand, and after that I got back to finishing everything off.

By the time I went to put my tools away in the shed although, my body was aching in all kinds of places, and I felt like I could have fallen asleep by only leaning up against the shed wall. And when I came back across the lawns to my new flower-beds, to have a look at them finished to see what I thought, I had to sit down there in the grass, or otherwise I thought I might have fallen down. And I stayed on by sitting there for a while, long after I had finished looking at my work.

But guess what happened while I was there, although; while I was just gathering the energy together to get me back to my quarters. What it was, Frank came down to where I was sitting, and he stood there right beside me, just looking. And then, after a little while he even sat down in the grass beside me.

I was too tired to become as tight as I usually would have although, with Frank sitting right there. But he did sit on beside me for a good long time, without even saying anything at all, and I did become just as uncomfortable as my exhaustion would allow. Mainly all I really wanted to do anyway was just go back to my quarters by then, and lie down for a while before I had something to eat. But Frank kept on just sitting there and not saying anything, and no matter how I tried to will him away it wouldn't work any. He just kept on staying. And then, at last, he spoke.

"This is away beyond what I expected," he said. "And I'll be honest with you too, when you first started here I was a bit . . . doubtful. And I said so to Elizabeth too. I mean you're not . . . But that's as it might be. You can certainly do what matters, and you've made a beautiful job of everything here so far."

He turned his head towards me quite suddenly then, and I think he must have saw how I flinched. But all he did was nod slowly and then look back to my flowers again. And then, after some more long quietness, and when I was thinking about simply going back to my quarters anyway, he began to speak again.

"So I'll tell you what," he said. "Most evenings, when Elizabeth and I are both finished working for the day, we stay behind for a while and have a little drink in our staff room up there. So come on up just now and I'll set one up for you too. And no arguments either, it's no more than you deserve."

And straight off, the very first thing I did was curse myself inside.

And for a moment, just because I was so very weary, I thought I was even going to weep without being able to hide any of anything.

The thing was, you see, all while I'd been working so hard and so long during the past few days, I'd forgotten all about my new suspicion. I hadn't hardly had any time at all to think about anything other than those stupid flower-beds, and I'd completely forgotten about how I'd begun to suspect that maybe some people can tell everything all about me, just by looking.

So all the while Frank had been there, I hadn't made any attempts at all to try and hide any of myself from him. And as he got up, and slowly began to climb the lawns, I felt certain that wherever we were going it wasn't to have a drink in his staff room.

He turned his head around again then and waved at me to follow him, and the truth of it was that I couldn't even think of anything else to do. Most other times I guess I would just have taken to my heels, right then, and I did think of it. But the thing was I couldn't. First of all I didn't have a penny of money saved anymore, and secondly it meant I would have to leave just everything behind this time, all unpacked in my little quarters.

And as I got tiredly to my feet the thought of having to go back to not even having a place like that made me just forget it, and I began to follow Frank a little behind. And as we climbed, my tiredness and my frightenedness all got mixed up in each other together, and the strangest of all was I began to think that, perhaps, even if Frank did make a horrible attempt to rip and tear me up, perhaps I wouldn't even try to run. Because I was just so sick inside, always of waiting, and it had been too much. And at least then I wouldn't have to wake to any more days of gardening, and I wouldn't have to end up in another strange town with no emergency money saved. Or go without having any little quarters of my own, now that I knew how fine that was. So all I did, exhausted and afraid, was I decided just to follow after him. Wherever he led.

7

I wonder if you've got to thinking yet that I might be lunatic, or even maybe mad, with all my talk about waiting and all my fear about people and such. I just had the idea that maybe you really do think that, but it's only because I haven't told you any yet about the most important of Nalda's stories. And I didn't really mean to either, just in case you might decide to come on after me yourself. But since I've said nothing already about which city I could be in, or about my name, or even about what I look like, I suppose it would be almost safe. Just so's as you don't think I'm only a lunatic man.

Or even mad.

Of all the stories I ever asked Nalda for, you see, the ones which I asked her for most of all, and almost every day, were the ones about my father. She had a huge amount of those, and they were always the most exciting of all, because of the job my father had. Because the thing was, for the greater part of his life, my father was a jewel thief.

And that's the true thing.

He worked with a very large team of people, my father. A large team who all plotted and planned for long periods of time between each operation. But it was always him, alone, who carried the whole thing out when they were ready. It was him who took all the risks. And that was why I always asked Nalda to say so much about him.

There were stories where he came so close to being caught that no matter how many times I asked for the same one I always believed, before the end, that this time he really wasn't going to escape. And there were ones too where, after finding out about what could terrify a certain guard, the only weapons he brought along might be three match-boxes, each with a real live spider inside. And he would conduct his business using only those.

The thing about most of Nalda's other stories although, the ones not about my father, was that they mostly all had their own special place where I would ask for them, and where Nalda would tell about them. Like, with the story about the silver ring and the fish, I would only ask for that and Nalda would only tell it either when it was on our way home from working, or else when we were sitting out on our sofa in the evenings. Then the story about her sunset friend, she would only ever tell about that when we were working in Mr. Michael's garden. But with the stories about my father, they were different. I would ask for those and Nalda would tell them just about anywhere. Just so long as there was no one else around to be listening in.

She also sometimes told me a little about my mother too, Nalda, and of how she had always been afraid and disapproving of what it was my father did to live. Every time my father went out to complete a job, Nalda said, my mother would always make him promise that this was his last one, and that when it was over he would turn to something new. And he always would promise too. And then, almost just as soon as the job was finished he would line up straight away for another one, and then it all began again.

But then one night, Nalda said, my father came home from completing a job to find that my mother was gone, and that she had gone forever.

"And beside the lamp," Nalda told me, "she had left a note for your father. And all it had on it was four words, which said, 'Too much is enough.' And in the corner of the room, you were still there, all alone, and fast asleep in your cot."

But Nalda didn't know much more than that about my mother. She didn't ever know her very much at all. And so it was only my father that we mostly talked about. And there was one story in particular which I just always asked for, and which was the most important one of all. And that was the story of why I'd come to be in Nalda's charge, besides of how.

It all happened about a year after my mother had gone away for good, Nalda said, when my father was starting to get tired. And, by then, it had become so that if he wasn't working, all he would do was just tend to me. And then for the rest of the time he would only just sit up by the window with me in his arms, watching the sky.

We didn't live in a big house, Nalda said. And we weren't rich either; there were far too many other people involved with my father's business for that to be possible. But in his weariness my father had begun to think of better things. Of a better house; of being richer; of a better way of living for me. And it was during those times, while he sat watching the sky in the evenings with me in his arms, that he began to hatch his plan.

He had been unhappy for a long time about the way the money from each job was divided up. There were men who made much more than him without ever having to take a single risk, and without ever even having to leave the hideaway sometimes. So first of all he'd decided that he wouldn't take part in any more jobs until he'd got that straightened out. But somewhere along the way, Nalda supposed, some evening as he rocked me gently by the window and stared out at the stars, he must have decided just to keep his mouth shut about it all, in case anyone should suspect he had any grievances about the way things were. And then, instead, what he decided to do was this:

The job that was being planned for next time was to be their biggest one from all and ever, for a jewel so rare and so precious it far outweighed anything they had ever taken before. So my father attended every meeting faithfully and showed no signs of anything to anyone. And when the time came, he carried out the whole operation just exactly as it had been planned and he carried it out successfully, without a hitch. But then, instead of returning to the meeting place with the stone, what he did was come straight to where he'd left me with a friend, and all through that night he drove us far and away, to an old abandoned cottage in a country field, which he'd been stocking up for a long time in advance.

We stayed there for a long time, Nalda told me. Maybe even a few months. And what my father had planned to do was remain in hiding for a while, and then sell the stone secretly elsewhere, to take us off to a country where we would both be safe and rich. But something went wrong somehow, and my father soon learned that both the law and the men he had tricked were now looking for both him and the stone. And as well as there now being little chance that anyone would buy the diamond when it was so wanted, it would also have been too dangerous for my father to even try to sell it to anyone, in case they should turn him in. And all he could do then was just sit with me in the little abandoned cottage, as our food ran down and my father's pursuers closed in, a little bit more every day.

"Picture him now," Nalda would say when we got to that bit every time. "Picture him sitting sweating in the falling-down cottage, with one of the most precious stones in the world hidden deep in his trouser pocket, and both his eyes fixed constantly on the door. Picture him struggling to try and think of some way to salvage at least something from the situation, as you slept soundly in his trembling arms. Picture him dirty and unshaven, with his hair in disarray and his confusion lined on his brow. And then, when you have all of that fixed, picture yourself slowly waking up and beginning to cry hungrily, and watch the sudden light of an idea as it spreads itself across his face."

His chasers were close by then, Nalda said, and he knew it. He could feel them. But he worked quickly. He laid me down on the bed, still crying, and then he went to the cupboard where the last of our food was stored. There wasn't much left, some moulded bread and a little milk, but he brought it all out in a hurry and carefully picked the worst mould from out of the bread. Then, after pouring the milk into a cup, he took the stone from the pouch in his pocket and folded it into the best pieces of the bread. And he fed it to me like that, between long gulps of milk.

A few moments later, when the only friend in the world that he could still trust arrived to tell him that his chasers were almost there, he gave the friend orders to deliver me safely to his sister, Nalda, with word of what he had done. And he took himself off across the fields, without much chance of ever getting anywhere.

And one day later, after a long journey by car again, I came to be with Nalda—maybe while she was out coaxing her roses to grow in the springtime, or maybe along a road white with freshly fallen snow. But certainly in a complicated array of rags and tatters, silent and afraid.

So that's the truthful and most important thing: my father was a jewel thief. And that's what keeps me always in waiting, and what keeps me so afraid and constantly in a state of such panic. Because, you see, the jewel is still right there inside of me. And I live caught between the thought of how fine life will be when it finally passes into my possession, and the fear that before it happens someone will slit me open to have it for their own.

That's the reason for why I've most always fled from a place the moment I've let just anything at all slip to anyone. Because of how I know about people, and about how all but the very few would rip up anything to get to the part which will bring them a profit or gain. And that's exactly what I thought Frank had in mind as he led me away that way, and up the lawns towards the building. That's exactly what I thought he had planned.

"Through here," he said, touching the top of my back with his hand, when we came to two doors which met each other in the middle and had glass in the top part. "We're almost there."

Already we had come down a corridor all grey and shining, with a smell I remembered from when I first came to see the woman who employed me. And after those doors we went along a narrower corridor where the smell wasn't quite so strong, and where it all wasn't quite so shiny, until we came to a yellow door joined on in the wall. And there Frank stopped and had me stop too, and after doing a wink at me he leant upon the handle and pushed it down.

It made me kind of jump some when the door opened full, because of the voice coming out from inside saying, "Well, well. Indeed now . . ." And another noise too, which was a television. But Frank put a hand around and up onto my shoulder and guided me into the room, and then he leant on the handle from the inside to close up the door.

So that was when I learned that Elizabeth was the same person as the woman who employed me, and she was sitting with her feet stretched on a chair doing a smile while I stood there.

"Well, well . . ." she said again, and I decided they must be both in it together, and that maybe it was even Elizabeth who had been able to see about me and not Frank at all.

"Sit down," Elizabeth said to me then. "Sit down now." And she herself got up and crossed to the TV, to turn its sound down some, while Frank asked me what I would like to drink, from over at this little cabinet he had gone to.

"Port?" he said, and as I sat down shakily, confused by all their moving about in the tiny little room, I saw him and Elizabeth doing a smile to each other, and I began to wonder of how much it would all hurt.

"There you go," Frank said to me, putting a glass down on the low table in front of me, and I jumped at the noise it made and Frank smiled some again.

"He's done a fine job," he said to Elizabeth. "Very fine indeed." And after he had sat down a bit further along the room, Elizabeth came back to sit down too. But instead of sitting in the same chair again she moved along to a one right beside of me, and made me become even more tightened.

They had a glass each too, her and Frank, and for a little bit they just drank from them and didn't say any things, while I stared at the pictures on the TV screen. But then it was that the woman who employed me leaned even a little bit closer to me, and she said, quite quietly, "Doesn't it make you feel very . . . special. Having such . . ." And just while my terror was growing very quick she suddenly made a gasp and stopped, and asked what had happened to my hand.

"I . . . I just . . . On some thorns," I said, and then Frank leaned in closer too, to have a look.

"That'll be alright," he said, once he had lifted my hand up and studied on it. "I'll just get something to clean it up with, and some cream. Then we'll cover it up and it should be fine in a few days' time."

So that was what he did, he took some things from a box hanging up on the wall and he saw to it very carefully. And while he was working on it and I was holding my arm all tightly and stiffly he did a smile at me and said, "Relax a little. It's not as if we're about to cut you up and eat you or anything . . ."

And Elizabeth laughed beside me.

Then Frank noticed that my glass was still sitting untouched and he told me to take a drink from it.

"It'll do you good," he said. And Elizabeth added that there was nothing else like it.

"In moderation, of course," she said.

So I picked it up with my hand all kind of shaking it some, and I took a gulp of it down, sure it was a thing to knock me out.

"There we are," Frank said, releasing my other hand. "That should do the trick." And as I coughed a bit and waited for it to happen he took his things back to the box on the wall and Elizabeth moved in closer to me again.

"Mind you," she said. "I don't suppose it's such a big price to pay. A little cut now and then. I'll tell you what I really envy you, I envy you the beauty your efforts produce. It must give you a real sense of satisfaction at the end of each day, to be able to stand back and appreciate what your work has produced. You must be very contented."

"He has a gift . . ." Frank said, closing the door of his box on the wall. "A real gift." And then he flipped through the channels on the TV for a while before returning it back to the one it had been at in the first place, all the while leaving the sound away down quiet.

"What my work here mostly involves," he said then, turning away from it, "is overlooking the caretaking staff, the cleaners, the porters, the maintenance people—and yourself of course. As far as Elizabeth is concerned, she mainly overlooks the people who keep things running. The kitchen people, the laundry staff—that side of things. Both of our jobs are pretty much thankless, and it's difficult to stand back and in any way be able to comprehend the results . . ."

"Whereas you . . ." Elizabeth said quietly, and then she took her rolled-up handkerchief out from inside her sleeve and wiped it along the bottom of her nose. "The past few gardeners we've had here," she said, "they did what they were asked to do competently enough, but no more. Just exactly what it took for them to get by, and that entirely without imagination. I've found that to be the case with most people though, really."

"That's it," Frank said. "But then, that's people for you. Ask them to make a mess of things, or destroy something, and they'll never let you down. But whenever it comes to . . . improvement . . ."

He shook his head.

"Anyway," Elizabeth said, and she tucked the handkerchief back in below her sleeve and got up from her chair. "That'll do me for tonight. But we want to see a lot more of you up here in future." And while I was staring at the TV I watched her taking her jacket from a hook and pulling it on, just out of my corners.

"Oh, of course . . . Yes," she said. "You don't have one of those down there in that little place, do you? Well, anytime, any evening—just wander up here." Then she discussed a few things with Frank, said "Good night" to both of us, and went home.

I was more than anything just confused by then. All the time I had been concentrating on every one of Frank and Elizabeth's movements, concentrating on Frank moving backwards and forwards from that little box on the wall and on just exactly everything he took out from inside it. And on how close to me and how far away Elizabeth kept moving. And when she'd gotten out of her seat I hadn't been sure of what exactly was going to happen, but the last thing in the world I would have guessed was for her just to leave.

So then I got to wondering again if maybe it was just Frank after all, and if he had only been waiting for her to go. But almost as soon as Elizabeth had gone he started getting himself ready too. Firstly he washed up his glass and Elizabeth's glass in the little sink there. Then he turned them upside down beside it and got his own jacket down.

So, even more confused, I got out of my own chair and took a single step towards the door. But as soon as I did Frank told me to sit myself right back down again, and I thought that here it was about to come now, and I grew very warm and very tight.

"No rush," Frank said. "No rush at all. Finish off your drink and everything. In fact, feel free to take another if it suits you. And I'm going to give you a key for this room here, so's you can watch some of that TV in peace and relax a little. And like Elizabeth said, just anytime . . ."

He asked me for my key-ring then, and when I gave it to him he added another new key to my collection.

"All I ask," he said, "is that you won't abuse the privilege. Help yourself to a drink, sure. But don't overdo it. I trust that you won't do anyway. Most people I wouldn't trust with all of this. People can be strange. But I have a feeling that you're a bit different . . ."

And he moved around the room for a few more minutes and turned the sound on the TV up for me. Then he just said "Good night" too, and reminded me to turn off the lights, the television, and lock the door before I left.

●

I sat for a while after that just surprised, I think, and all full of a sort of strange lightness too. Then, although, I got this other idea that maybe

47

it was both of them who were in it after all, but that neither of them were keen to do what was required. So maybe what it was, I thought, maybe they had just set me up in that room there, and now they had gone off to give someone else the signal, and they could split everything up three ways and go unsuspected. So I began waiting again, and listening quietly for a noise. But no one came.

No one did.

It seemed very strange to me, by then, and the only idea I could have was that I must have been wrong. I even thought back over some of the things Elizabeth and Frank had said while they'd been there. And the thing I remembered most was what they'd said about people, about how most people were. And that got me to thinking finally that maybe Elizabeth and Frank were of those other kind of people that Nalda had said of: those kind like us, who wouldn't rip and tear. The very few.

So I just sat back for a time wondering over that, and taking little sips on my glass while the TV went on, and gradually my scaredness went mostly away. And when it had, and I was watching this thing on the TV which was making me laugh some, I realised that the curious feeling of angriness and things from before Frank had even come down had mostly gone away too. They had mostly disappeared. And instead I had this good feeling, this feeling that maybe Frank and Elizabeth could turn out to be my friends or something. And once the thing I had been laughing at on TV had finished and I had turned it off, I washed my glass out at the sink, and just before I turned the light out I looked at it sitting upside down beside theirs, and somehow that made me feel even better too.

Then I locked up the door and made my way back down to my own little quarters, like I'd earlier thought I would never do again.

8

*T*he first thing I did next morning, as soon as I went out into the garden, was look around for something that needed doing up close to the hospital building. I had this idea that if I worked up close to there I might bump into Frank or Elizabeth some time through the day, and then they could maybe stop to be my friend for a while, or even say again of how it would be alright for me to come up to that little room again in the evening. So I looked around until I decided that the vines clinging to the walls of the hospital needed some work doing, and then I went down to get the tools I would need to do it.

The only one of them I saw throughout that whole day although was Frank, carrying a big box out through the main doors, and he didn't hardly stop to speak to me any at all. I stopped what I was doing as soon as I saw him, and waited until he noticed me too. But he seemed to be in quite a rush when he went past and all he did was just wink his eye at me and say, "There he is now. How are things?"

And while I said, "Yes"—in a funny sort of voice—he just hurried on and away, and he soon disappeared around the side of the building.

It made me feel quite sad when that happened, and I got sadder too as the time went on and I still didn't see any more of them. But then I made this other and different discovery, while I was still working up there, and that got me to feeling better again.

Every afternoon, you see, just after lunch times, some of the nurses bring some of the patients out onto the benches up at the hospital building. And while I was still working on those new flower-beds I sometimes used to watch them doing that, and watch how they helped some of them out on sticks and wheeled some of them out in chairs.

But what I hadn't never noticed before, because I'd always been so much further down and away, was that one of the nurses who helps them out is just about the most beautiful girl from ever. And that was the discovery I made that day.

She has this dark, dark hair, all tied up careful beneath her nurse's hat, with some long parts with loops which escape and fall out onto her shoulders. And while I was working I couldn't help but watch how she sometimes did a blush or a shy smile whenever one of the patients said something to her that I couldn't quite hear. And I couldn't help but feel good to think that from then on, at just about the same time every day, I'd be able to see her there, exactly like I'd thought would never happen here. But the only thing is, even although I will be able to see her like that, I don't think I'll be able to work quite as closely to her as that ever again, because of a crazy thing that happened while I was up there.

Every time the nurses bring those patients out, you see, there's this one they wheel out in a chair who always does the same thing, every time. And what it is, whenever the nurse who wheels him out positions his chair between the two benches, he always shakes his head slowly and then points ahead of him, and over some to the side too. And he keeps on by doing that until his nurse takes his brake off again, and wheels him a little distance away to where he can sit on his own, away from all the others.

Sometimes, while I was still doing those back-breaker flower-beds, I used to watch him doing that each time from down and away. And I watched how, if anyone ever shouted a question to him from over on the benches, he would only just shake his head to himself and look quite angry. Then he would only lift his hand in a way to tell them just to leave him alone, still sitting with his back to them all. So sometimes I would think he was just a little bit like me, that one, in how he always stayed away from folks.

Anyway, while I worked on those vines I was moving a little bit closer in the direction of where the nurses and patients were sitting always, but I was moving so slowly I knew I would never end up by being all that close to them. The one who doesn't ever like to sit with them, although, he was pushed away out to the same side of them as I was on, and quite far away from the wall. And, eventually, it got to be that I was working directly behind his chair, except I didn't know about that until I heard his shouting. And that was only what made me know.

I was only just working away, you see, and occasionally sneaking a spy at the special nurse—too fast for her to see me—when I heard the one in the chair making quite a loud noise. And it was when I turned around to look at him then that I saw I was just behind him.

I still didn't know it was me he was shouting at although. I didn't know that until the time when he shouted again. And when I turned around that time he was twisting his neck right round far, and staring at me.

"Don't you hear me, man?" he said quite loud. "Don't you hear? How are your biscuits?"

And all I could only do was frown at him, until he shouted again. And even then I couldn't make any sense.

"Pick me one down now!" he cried. "From your biscuits. Bring me the fruit. Bring me the fruit."

And while I stood there, all and confused, one of the other nurses came over to the old man in the chair and told him to leave the gardener alone. And as she said something to me, that I didn't hear properly, all I did was just gather my tools up together in a great hurry, and run off at a top speed all the way down the lawns and into my sheds.

So that's for why I won't never be able to work in a close place like that whenever they're all out again. Because of how I would always be scared that he was just about to shout at me again, and that I was just about to run away in such a same crazy way—to make the especial nurse think that I was truly a lunatic.

Or even mad.

I have seen her up close on one other time since then although, when none of those other people were around. And I don't know if you'll believe it or not, but the truth is that she even spoke to me then.

What it was, on the next day after all of that thing had happened, I went up to finish off those vines very early in the morning. And while I was up there Elizabeth came out through the main doors, just in exactly the same way Frank had done on the day before. I didn't get my hopes up about her stopping any to be my friend like I had done with Frank although, because I could see she was hurrying off towards those other doors in just the same way as he had done. But then, while I was turning around, she glanced to the side some and she saw me there. And then she stopped and she came back along.

"Good morning," she said to me. "You know, you were working away so quietly I almost didn't notice you were there. How are you?"

And I put my clipping tool down by my side and I nodded my head. And I said, "Yes."

"It's a strange mist that's hanging around this morning," Elizabeth said, while she looked along towards the doors she had been going to, and then she tapped her fingers some on this box she was carrying. "Listen," she said. "I've just got to go along there for a moment, but I'll see you when I come back out again, okay? I'll only be a few minutes, so don't run off." And then she went off to those doors, and I sat down on one of the benches for a little while—to wait.

It made me feel good when that happened, and took away the sadness I'd got when Frank only rushed on past the day before. But the thing was, when Elizabeth came back out again she had the very especial nurse with her, and that made me get very shy. They walked slowly along the path towards my bench, talking some to each other of things I couldn't hear, and then when they reached to where I was they mostly stopped and Elizabeth did me a smile.

"So where did you get to last night?" she asked me. "Frank and I were expecting to see you up in the little room."

And all I just did was touch the handle of my clipping tool against my stomach, and I said of how my stomach had been hurting some. But because of how I could feel the special nurse looking at me my voice came out all very strange, and I got even more shy.

"That's not so good," Elizabeth said. "And how are you feeling now?"

"Better," I said, and that got her to be looking a bit happier.

"Well, we'll expect to see you tonight again," she said. "There's no sense in sitting away down there all on your own. No sense at all."

And I thought they were maybe just about to go away then, and so did Elizabeth too I think, because she started to move off towards the main doors. But that was when the special nurse spoke to me, like I've already said of before. And instead of moving in the way Elizabeth was going she moved a little bit closer to the bench where I was sitting on, and then she began to speak in a very smooth and warm voice.

"I'm sorry about what happened yesterday," she said. "With old Will. But you really needn't take too much notice of him. He's really quite harmless."

And Elizabeth came back closer and asked what all this was about.

"It was just old William," the nurse said. "I think he gave the gardener something of a fright yesterday, shouting nonsense at him while he was working."

"Oh, he's completely mad," Elizabeth said to me, and did another smile. "Round the bend—don't worry about that at all."

And they did start to go back to the main doors then, both of them together, and after Elizabeth had said again that she would see me in the evening, and after the doors had swung closed and they had both disappeared, I just sat amazed for a while. Amazed to think of how the beautiful nurse had just spoken to me.

9

I wasn't making any lies when I said to Elizabeth of how my stomach had been hurting on that night before, even although it wasn't the reason for why I didn't go up any. But lots of times, especially on nights, my stomach gets to hurting very bad, like as if my diamond is moving around in there and getting closer to coming out. And even although it hurts so much sometimes that all I can do is just lie down on my side with my knees pressed in hard against my stomach, it still makes me get excited too, because of how I know it means my diamond is getting ever closer. And it will soon be mine for sure.

The other thing about it, although, is that when I finally get to sleep like that, it always gives me the strangest of dreams. And it gave me a very strange one on that night too.

What it was, I was up working on the vines like I had been on that afternoon, and the old man in the chair shouted at me in it too. But when I turned around to look at him this time it all turned out that it wasn't him who was there in the chair, but it was Nalda instead. And she was shouting just like he had been, but louder and more. And spitting too, like she really did do when I got to be older and more grown.

In my dream although, I said the same thing to her as I used to say when she only started to shout, when I was still very young. I knelt down to the side of her chair and I whispered, "Say about us to me, Nalda. Tell about the ring . . ." But, in my dream, it was like how it was one time when I was older. She didn't even be like she knew who I was, while she was shouting. And then, suddenly, she turned back into the old man and he started shouting some of his same crazy things again.

It was a strange kind of a dream for sure. And through all the next day, after Elizabeth and the special nurse had spoken to me up at those vines, I kept on by thinking of it now and again, and I kept on by thinking of other things about Nalda too. But the main thing I kept thinking about, most of all, was just going up to see Elizabeth and Frank in that little room when it got to be evening, and my happiness about that just kept on by getting bigger and bigger as the day moved on.

I didn't do any work that was too difficult after I moved away from the vines, mostly because I was still a bit weak after my stomach being so sore. All I did really was just tidy up some of the plants which climb up on the back wall. And when it was finally time for me to finish up for the day, I went back to my little quarters to have something to eat and to wash up a bit. And then, excitedly, I climbed the sloping lawns to the hospital building, and followed through all the doors and corridors that Frank had first shown me through.

I even had my keys out in my hand too, in case it should be that the door for the room would be locked, and I would be first there. But when I got to it I could hear voices and the TV inside, so I only just knocked on the door and then I watched the handle until it moved down, and the door began to open.

"Ah ha!" Frank said when he saw it was me, and he pulled the door open wider. "Come in, come in. Elizabeth has just been telling me all about your trouble with old Will." And as I wobbled into the room Elizabeth did me a smile, then took the handkerchief out from in her sleeve and wiped along her mouth with it.

"Have a piece of cake," she said to me. "Someone brought it for one of the patients, but they don't like cake—so they gave it to me. It's very nice."

She put a piece on a plate and laid it down on the table in front the chair I'd chose, and Frank took another piece for himself.

"How about some port too?" he asked me, and he poured a glass and put it down beside the cake.

"Now," he said, "let's hear all about old Will. I always like to keep abreast of his utterances. I'm convinced there's a strange wisdom in there, if only you can interpret them properly."

Elizabeth laughed and put her handkerchief back inside of her sleeve.

"I think you must be as crazy as he is, Frank," she said. "Or maybe more so. At least he knows he's just mad."

I picked my glass up carefully and took a drink from it while it shook some. Then I looked at the smile Frank was doing and said, "Biscuits."

But when I did that his smile turned into a frown some, and I blushed and grew a little bit afraid.

"That's . . ." I said in a quavery kind of voice, "That's what the old man said of."

And I watched Frank's frown while it smoothed out mostly, before I said anything else. Then I told him, "He said, 'How are your biscuits, my man?' That's what he said of."

And Frank began to laugh a bit crazily, kind of as if he was coughing very loudly in a way.

And I said, "He asked me to pick him one down."

"One what?" Frank asked in gasps of breath between his laughing.

"I . . . mostly I don't know. But I think he meant about biscuits."

Elizabeth even started to laugh too then, and Frank got a bit like as if when Nalda tickled me sometimes—gasping between his coughing and trying to stop. And I got excited a bit, I think, and I started by talking quite fast then.

"I didn't even have any biscuits," I said. "And then he started off by shouting out, 'Get me some fruit, my man. Get me some fruits.' "

Frank hit the air with his hands then, with his face red, and gasping, "Please, no . . ."

And I started to laugh too. And then I thought it must have been a long, long number of years since I'd laughed with other people, and an even longer time since it was something I said that made them laugh, except when they were just laughing at what I said, and pulling fun. And I got to be quite excited really. I said it all again, about the biscuits and the fruit, speaking quite fastly. And I said about how the old man in the chair had looked, and I even made some bits up about him shaking his fist in the air and things, to keep them laughing for longer. And Elizabeth took her spectacle glasses off and pushed her hands onto her eyes, to try and stop the tears that were running out while she laughed—mostly at Frank I think really. And at the way he looked like he was trying to push away an invisible ghost who was tickling him always.

Eventually, although, we did stop laughing some. And after wiping her handkerchief along on her eyes, Elizabeth put her glasses back on, and Frank's face came back to being its normal colour and he got his breath back a bit and I stopped talking about the old man then.

What I did say although, still quite excited even after the laughter had gone away, was "I had a dream last night where Will turned into Nalda, while he was shouting." Without even really thinking. And as Elizabeth poured herself some more port into a glass she asked who Nalda was, and I said quickly that she was my aunt.

"I used to live with her some, once," I added on after that, and then I picked up my cake and did a big bite to stop myself from saying any more stupid things. Just in case I slipped something out which would suddenly mean I had to move on—just when I was almost getting to be happy. And to have friends.

Later on from there, when Frank and Elizabeth had been talking to each other about work things for a while, and I had been watching quiet pictures on the TV screen, Frank finally poured out a glass of port for himself and he sat down and sighed like just everything was fine. And then a great big grin broke across his face, and he laughed a little bit again.

"I don't want you to think," he said to me. "I don't want you to think that I find old Will's situation funny in any way. Not at all. In a lot of ways it's a sad and terrible thing. But, ah . . . We laughed good tonight."

And he did a grin and looked to Elizabeth.

"Didn't we?" he said to her. " 'How are your biscuits, my man?' Jesus." And they both of them laughed and I joined in too—although probably a bit too loudly this time, just because of how I didn't really have a laugh there at that time, and I had to make one up.

"Still," Frank continued, "it is important to laugh well sometimes. Especially when your work leaves you with as little to laugh about as mine or Elizabeth's usually does."

Elizabeth nodded in agreement, and then, after drinking out all that was left in her port, she rinsed her glass around under the tap and turned it upside down beside the sink.

"All the same, Frank," she said as she tidied up a few things in the room, and then took her coat down from off its hook. "You always have your horses, eh? Maybe one of those complicated bets will pay off one day and you'll have nothing left to worry about here."

And as she said "Good night" to us both and then disappeared, Frank got up to wash his own glass and he said quietly to me, "Well, let's hope so . . ."

"It's all that keeps me going a lot of the time," he said while the tap gushed. "I know it might seem strange to someone like you, someone who's as dedicated to their work as you are, and who gets just as much back from it too. But most days, I'm afraid, it's only the hope that one of the bets I place each morning will pay off that gets me through the day."

And afterwards, after Frank had gone too and I was enjoying a little bit of the television, I felt sure that if he hadn't begun a long description of his betting techniques at that moment, and of the way it would all add up if it ever came together properly . . . I knew for sure that if he hadn't suddenly confused me with all of that I would have said to him, "But that's just like me too."

I had been all ready to let it slip out, and then it would have made me have all kinds of trouble. And a terrible mess.

And as I took another piece of the cake I thought about how lucky I'd been, and about how careful I was going to have to be whenever I got all excited again.

10

So that's about how things have been here for about the past two weeks mostly. I've spent some time almost every night up in that little room with Elizabeth and Frank. And sometimes I've only been there for a few minutes to ask some bits about the garden, and other times I've spent nearly even two hours listening and talking, and watching the pictures on the TV screen. Mostly although it's about half of an hour, or a full one, and the thing is—the most amazing thing—I've begun to think that sometimes when I'm there I talk a little bit just too much.

Always throughout the days now I watch out for things that would be good to tell Elizabeth and Frank when I next see them. Things I think will make them laugh or interest them. Or amaze them some. And sometimes, too, when I'm with them I start by talking all about one thing and then I think of all kinds of others while I'm still speaking, and I go right onto them after.

It's a bit like, since I haven't had anyone to talk to for so much of a time, it's all started to come out at once now. And laughing is the best thing of all. Like having other people make you laugh, and then making them laugh some, and all laughing in together too. I forget even how long it is since I laughed like that before. But Frank was right that time, it is very important. And up until about four days ago I was thinking always on how it was the very best thing that had ever once happened to me since Nalda went away. And on how nothing other than the arrival of my jewel could possibly make me feel more happier. But let me say now about a thing which has happened just over the past few days, and which for me is maybe even more especial.

There was an afternoon, you see, just four days ago now, when I was out doing some watering of the flower-beds because of how it had been so dry for so long. And because I hadn't much felt like setting up all of the hose, or the sprinklers or any like that, I was only just using a sprinkling can; filling it up when it needed to be filled at the tap on the side of the shed.

While I was doing all of that although, Elizabeth came down the lawns with this very frail old lady who leaned on a stick, and they both of them just stood quietly beside me while I poured water out onto the flowers and the soil.

"This is Maude," Elizabeth said out to me after a while, and she winked her eye at me secretly when I turned round to look at the old lady. "She's been pestering me to bring her down here for days now, haven't you, Maude?"

But the old lady only just did a kind of smile and looked quietly at one of the flowers.

"She loves flowers," Elizabeth said. "Don't you, Maude?"

And in this faint little cracked voice, almost a bit like mine comes out sometimes, the old woman said, "I once had a very beautiful garden . . ." And she looked at me quickly, then she looked at my sprinkling can and she said, "Could I?"

I looked to Elizabeth then, and Elizabeth nodded. So I let the old lady take the handle of the can while I supported its weight from the bottom, because of how I knew she was just too frail to be able to lift it all up herself. And when it was that she tried to tip it I lifted it up at the back, so that the water sprinkled out onto one of the flowers. Then, after the flower was soaked, I let it fall back and the old lady shuffled along the edge of the flower-bed with her stick in one hand and the handle of the can in the other. And when she came to a stop again I tipped the base forward once more and we soaked another flower.

"Alright now . . ." Elizabeth said when we had soaked over quite a few of them. "Let's us get back up now, Maude, and leave the gardener to his work." And she did a smile at me. But her idea didn't really make Maude much too happy although. I saw her little hand tighten around the sprinkling can and she said, in her same frail and quiet voice from before, "Oh . . . Just a few more flowers. Just a few more minutes, Elizabeth. Please . . ."

"Well . . ." Elizabeth said. "I have things to do now, Maude."

"But please," Maude said. "Just a few more flowers."

"Well," Elizabeth said. "I'll tell you what. I have to go, but I'll send Marie down on my way up. Will she be alright with you for a few minutes?" Elizabeth asked to me, and I shrugged some. "Alright," she said. "You're an old pest, you know, Maude." But Maude only just looked at me and drew in her tiny little shoulders, and did a smile with her tiny pin-point eyes shining. Then we moved onto the next flower.

The thing was, although, when Marie came down into the gardens it turned out that Marie was the nurse who always makes my heart go fast and slow. And when I saw her coming down through the lawns I got so very nervous that all I could do was just stare at the flowers we were sprinkling as hard as Maude was doing, and pretend to be just as occupied with them too.

"Hello, Maude," the nurse said when she got down to where we were, and she stood on the opposite side of Maude from where I was. "Causing trouble again?" And as I turned around secretly to spy at her quickly she did a smile to me behind Maude—and the thing was, when I tried to do a smile back to her, it worked! I don't really know how, but it just did anyway. And then I stared back to the flowers again and we moved along onto the next one.

"You've been very good with her," the nurse said to me after a little while. "Very patient, though I suppose you need a lot of patience to do what you do. With so much watching and waiting."

And when she said that I just about almost jumped out of my skin, before I saw she meant gardening, and not the other thing I do. Just for a second although I'd had the feeling that she knew all about me, when she said that. And it took me a few moments to get a hold of myself back quite quickly again, and then I only just nodded.

"It might. Maybe," I said, and the nurse did that shy smile looking at the flowers, the one I'd always seen before when she was with the patients. Then she lifted her head up again, and she looked around some and said, "It is a beautiful garden. It had become so neglected I'd stopped noticing, but you've made it very beautiful again, hasn't he, Maude?"

And Maude looked at me and said, "I once had a very beautiful garden."

And then her smile faded.

"I'm tired . . . Marie," she said, and she tried to lift the can up to me and I took the handle.

"Had enough now?" the nurse said to her. "Alright then. You've done very well, Maude. But we'll get back up now. Say thank you to the gardener." And Maude did her crazy little smile to me again.

"Thank you," the nurse said instead. Then they made a slow journey back up the lawns, with the old lady leaning one hand on her stick and the other on the nurse's arm. And I watched after them for a while before I went across to the tap again to refill my sprinkling can.

So that's the even more especial thing which has happened, although not only. You see, for every day since then, just around about the same time, Marie brings Maude down into the garden. And while Maude spends a little time with pretending to be helping me, Marie stands alongside us while I help Maude, and she talks to me all about all of most things. I'm not so good at talking all to her yet, not so good as I can with Frank and Elizabeth at least. But I think I'm probably a bit better than I would have been from before, and my smile always keeps on by working to her, just about all of most times.

There are two things I keep noticing although. And one is the way she always suddenly says things that make me think all at once that she knows just all about me; that make me jump just all out of my skin, before I see I've only misunderstood again. Exactly like on that first time when she said about my patience and my waiting, and I didn't know that she only meant about my gardening.

This is the other thing too although. I've found out that I can't do lies to her like I can do to Elizabeth and Frank. And more than that also, because whenever she asks me something I find I can't even just get on by staying quiet, or by saying about something else instead. It seems, in fact, that I want her to know about things. About all kinds of things.

There was this time, just two days ago, when I had given Maude a little trowel, and we were all three of us kneeling down at the edge of a flower-bed while Maude dug some little holes and planted some little bulbs in. And while we were doing it, with me kneeling on one side of Maude, and Marie kneeling on the other, she said to me, "I remember doing this in school once, in the garden outside. But my flower didn't grow."

And before I even thought once I said all about how I never did go to school.

"Because of how they only make you be like all of everyone," I said. "And Nalda taught me reading and writing and sums herself. And time. And whenever the people came around who try and make you go to school she hid me away in a special place."

But the thing was although, Marie only laughed. That's my one stroke of luck. Because whenever it is that I tell her a true thing she says I'm just telling her a story, or that I'm teasing.

First of all when I told her about Nalda, and when I said of how I first came to her in a complicated array of rags, all silent and afraid, once she had laughed she made her eyes go all narrow to look at me, and she said, "You're very secretive."

Which is the strangest thing. But it's lucky also I suppose. Because of how it keeps me safe.

11

*I*n the evenings, meanwhile, Frank has been spending all lots of times explaining about his "little spark of hope" to me. Explaining about his methods he uses for always betting on horse races, and on the ways it would work out if he was to win. I found it all very difficult to understand at first, but I think I can just about follow now. Just about.

What it seems is, every day, through all the country, they have these races where all the horses try their best to beat each other over the end line. And, also, the main reason for it is that people bet money about which one will be first across. But these experts, they know how likely each of these horses is to win, in each race, and so each horse has a kind of number—its odds number. And the more likely it is to win then the lower the number, and the less likely it is to win then the higher. And however much money you bet, if your horse wins your money gets multiplied by that number, and that's how much you win. Sort of. Although not exactly. But that's how I think on it just now, anyway.

"You're going to drive the man crazy," Elizabeth said to Frank one night, as I sat beside him and struggled to understand about these example sums he was doing out on some paper. "He'll end up making you like old Will," Elizabeth said to me, and she began to laugh. "You'll end up wandering around shouting, 'How are your biscuits?' to strangers. That's what happened to Will, you know. He was only here with a broken arm to begin with, and then Frank started trying to explain all of this to him."

And we all laughed some, even Frank too, and then afterwards he said, "I'm only trying to give him an education."

It surprised Frank quite a lot when he found out at first that I didn't understand anything about any of it, and even Elizabeth thought it was quite unusual. But then, later, she said, "It's not so surprising, though, since he was brought up by a woman alone. Most women wouldn't waste their time with such nonsense."

And Frank said, "Of course they would. Everyone has something. It's essential."

And when I had a kind of understanding of how horses worked he explained his own special way of doing things to me.

"It's called accumulation," he said. "Each day I choose six horses, and I put on only a small stake—you're only ever in danger when you start raising your stake all the time. That's when you can really get into trouble."

So what happens with this accumulation thing, as Frank explained it, you pick out more than one horse and then they all of them have to win. And if they do then the money from the first is added . . . no, multiplied by the odds number of the second; then all of that is multiplied by the odds number of the third, and such like. And if the horses you had weren't much likely to win, and had high-up odds numbers, then it soon adds to be quite a big final number. And that's the money you get.

"The secret," Frank said, "is to pick some horses that are quite likely to win for your first few, so's your stake grows. And then, for your last couple, you pick some real outsiders—and if they come home then the outcome will be enormous."

Most people, Frank says, stick to all horses who are quite likely to win and then they do win quite often.

"But I'm not interested in winning just a few hundred pounds here and there," he said. "That wouldn't change anything. Not really. I haven't ever won anything yet, but when I do . . . I only have to win once. That's all it will take. It's faith that counts, just faith. That's all you need."

"What you need," Elizabeth laughed, "are some of those pills they give old Will to try and keep him balanced. That's what you need."

Now that he's explained all about it to me although, he insists that I place a bet of my own every now and again too, after his own method.

"You have to let the hope in," he told me, and he said, really, that I should place one every day—so's that every day the little bit of hope is there. But I told him that I couldn't afford it every day, because of how, like you know, I have no need of that hope. And also because of how, even if it did work out for me one time, it wouldn't really change anything much for me. Cause I would still have to live with my frightenedness. It's only the arrival of my diamond that can change things for me, because it's only then that I'll be free of the possibility that at any moment someone may rip me wide.

But anyway although, quite lots now the evenings see me sitting beside Frank at the table in that little room, studying the horses for the next day's races, and putting together my own combination just to make him do a smile. We only pick them by what their odds numbers are, and pay no attention to any past results or riders' names; all of which I don't understand about anyway. And Frank seems always very pleased when he looks over to the list I've made.

"That's the way," he says. Or else, "Now you're getting it." And Elizabeth does a joke that he's only so happy with me because I'm the only person he's ever been able to convince to try his method, and that I'm the only person in the whole of history who's ever paid him enough attention to be able to understand it, let alone put it into practice.

He paid me some extra special attention this morning although, because of a stupidness I made of myself last night, while we were choosing out our horses. I didn't know before, you see, that the place for putting your bets on horses is called a bookmaker's. And while I was with

Frank last night he called it by that name for the first time, and what I said back made him know that I thought he was talking about a place where people made books. To read. And then he knew that I hadn't never been to one. So he said that I had to go. And this morning, so's that I could, he gave me a little bit of time off from gardening, and he took me along with him to the place where he makes his bets each day.

We went in Frank's car to the place, and while he drove I held the betting slips we'd already filled in—both his and mine.

"Now," he said to me on the way there, "I shouldn't expect you'll actually like this place very much. It's important you should see it, but it probably won't be entirely pleasurable. They always tend to smell just slightly of desperation, these places."

I did like it a bit although. It wasn't quite so bad. It did smell some, of something, and all the people inside scared me a bit, but it wasn't so very bad. They had all of these TV screens, some with names of horses and their odds numbers on, and some with horses wandering around with all of their riders on. And they had a lot of pens lying around in there too, and Frank said I could take a couple home. Because of how I liked how small they were, not like usual pens. And I didn't even have to pay.

We stayed around to watch just one race on the TV screens in there, after Frank had given our slips and our money to a woman behind a window, but neither of us had one chosen in that race. And then we left.

"I don't like to spend too much time in there," Frank told me outside. "I don't like being able to feel everyone else's hope. And they all exasperate me anyway, those people. They have no plan most of them; they just throw money around and sometimes win and sometimes lose. And even when they do win they just put it all on another bet some other time and lose it all sooner or later. You can feel their hope, and really . . . it's just all a waste."

He talked a bit more about the people in there as we drove back, and then pointed out some places that we passed. One place had a whole lot of people around the outside that he said was a hall for this game where you have a card with numbers on, and someone shouts out a lot of numbers and if they're all on your card then you win a lot of money. And then this other kind of a place that he said was something called a casino, where people played all many different kinds of betting games.

"The way I see it," he said to me while we drove, "is that just about everyone is waiting for a special thing to happen to them. The thing that will change their life from being what it is into what they want it to be. And only the individual involved knows what that thing is. Or sometimes they don't. Sometimes they just have a vague sense of what it would be. But in most cases, except I suppose in the case of the very rich, money is a big part of the equation."

Then he looked at me out of his corners, and I grew to be a bit nervous.

"I know Elizabeth and I are forever talking about how contented and fulfilled gardening must make you," he said, "but it's my guessing that you have a faith of your own too. Am I right?"

And I think I must have begun to even look scared by then because he quickly said, "It's alright. Don't worry. I'm not about to ask you what it is. These can be very personal things, I know. I'm very open about my own, but I know other people might just as soon not want to talk about it. And I wouldn't expect them to. I would just be interested to know."

And I relaxed some again as we stopped for a minute at a light that was red, and I said, "Yes . . ."

"I knew it," Frank said, and did a big smile. "I knew it. I always like to think I can tell. That I can feel an affinity with those who are like me."

And when a green light came he started us moving again, then he pointed out another building.

"Look at the church there," he said to me. "I don't know if you'd agree or not, but to me that's no longer where faith belongs. What most people really want now—the way I see it—is a shot at what's on offer in life. Just look at the number of people gathered where we just were, and outside the bingo hall waiting. And look at the number of people frequenting the casinos on any night, or playing on lotteries. That's where people take their faith to now, and where they place their faith. The numbers visiting that building are very few in comparison now. It wasn't always the case, I know. But there's so much on offer in this life now, if only you have the means. Whereas, if you don't, it can be such a damn sad and sorry affair. Wouldn't you agree?"

I did a nod.

"An awful lot of the time," Frank said then, "it's only the belief that one day my horses will all come good, and that some of the things on offer will at last be available to me—a lot of the time that's the only thing that makes the present bearable to me. Isn't that the same with you?"

"It is," I said shyly. "Yes." And Frank did a big smile again.

"And it's the same with all of the people you saw in there too," he said. "Faith, that's the important thing. Perhaps there is a lot of pleasure to be had from a garden, and a lot to be learned there. But if it's not what you want . . . You have something of a gift for gardening, I could see that from the very beginning, but if you don't actually enjoy it . . ."

Then he stayed silent for a while as we drove back through the rest of the town. And I thought a little bit of how it would have been good to be able to tell him what it was I was waiting on. To prove to him I wasn't like those others he didn't like for having no real plan; by showing him the certainty there was that my waiting would pay. But also, too, I was glad that the way he had talked about us being the same meant he had no clue ever about me, and I was still safe to stay.

"Well, here we are again then," he said eventually, when we drove back through the gates of the hospital. "Back to reality for the time being. The great crippler."

And as he parked and stopped he asked of who could blame us for encouraging a little bit of light into the day, when it promised as little joy for us both at its outset.

69

12

But this is the thing, although. This is the secret. While Frank was driving me back from the betting place this morning, and while I admitted of how I was waiting for a prize which would take me away too, that really wasn't what was on my mind at all. And when we came back through the gates of the hospital, and Frank said neither of us had much of a day ahead of us, the true thing was that I was bristling for to get back to my garden. I was all full of a joy just to be thinking of getting down there and unlocking the sheds, and then working quietly and patiently at something until the part of the day when Maude and Marie would come down.

And so, here is another secret too. Here's something I've begun to do.

Just lately, over the last few days, I've begun to eat less, because of how it will mean I'll only have to use my can and do my searching on every second day, instead of every one. And that's because I'm actually afraid of my jewel arriving right just now, and putting all things to ruin.

It would have given me a big shock a little time ago, to know I'd be doing what I'm doing just now. Especially too since I know it's so close now. The pains I have now are sometimes very bad, the pains of my diamond moving around and down. A lot of times I spend out the whole night on my side, with my knees pulled up. And even sometimes too the pains come to me in the day now. And I whisper quietly to them. At night, lying on my bed, I say over and again, "Just a few days more. Don't come tomorrow. Just a few more days . . ."

And as I drift from sleep and out, I have dreams with myself in—weeping on a bus that rolls, with my jewel in a pouch in my pocket, off to sell it and move away. And I have dreams, too, where the boy with the pictures on his arms comes here, while I'm standing in the garden with Maude and Marie, and he chases me with his knife over the wall, and far through streets and fields, and on and away from here forever.

On the days when my pains get really bad, and I have to rush to use my can, I search very frightenedly now. Hoping always that nothing will be there, not just yet. And hoping that I can have one more day still in this garden. And when I find nothing I feel very relieved, and I get happy again. And I go back out into the garden with a feeling even like I used to have when Nalda first let me do a few things, and when it was her who had the angriness and the resentment, and the cut fingers and the sore bit on her back. And all I had was a happiness and an amazement because things grew and changed from each day and on. Like I kind of have again now.

●

But while I was out and waiting this morning, after we had come back, I got quite upset and worried. And the reason for why was because it began to rain some. It kept on right up through lunch time too, and none of the nurses or patients came out to any of the benches, not old Will nor any of those. And I even started to get angry at the rain, because of how much I had already looked forward into the day. And while I was working around I did a thing that I haven't never did before, not on any time. I got so angry and so unhappy that I hit a rose and broke the head off it, and I crushed it all up in my hand. Then I hid it all quickly away in the pocket of my coat and checked around to make sure no one had seen me do it.

No one had done although there was still no one else out in the garden or around the building, even although the rain had mostly stopped by then. But while I stood looking around I did see the main doors opening, and as I watched I saw it was Maude and Marie who came out. And before they could spy at me just standing around and not doing any things, I went back to what I'd been at before. I pretended to work while I watched the thing that has come to be what gets me through these new days, and those nights when my jewel is hurting: Marie slowly descending the lawns towards me, gently holding Maude's arm as Maude looks about excitedly with that crazy little smile on.

What I was working at was digging in these flowers close to the borders of some of the more older flower-beds, flowers that arrived in white trays yesterday. And I was kneeling with the trowel in my hand, packing earth all in hard round one of them, when Maude and Marie finally came to being where I was.

"Hello sir," Maude said when they stopped, and I thought of how strange a thing it was to say. And I thought, probably, that not anyone had ever called me sir before.

"Hello," Marie said too. "I hope we aren't beginning to get on your nerves like this every day. I thought maybe you'd get a rest when it was raining, but as soon as it stopped she wouldn't give me any peace. Eh, Maude?"

And Maude drew her little shoulders in.

"Isn't the joke beginning to wear thin for you yet though?" Marie asked to me. "You've already been more than patient, but if we're holding you back now . . ."

So I shook my head, and probably for longer than I should have too, but only because I was scared in case she might not bring them back any more times. And the true thing was I couldn't think of a worse way than that. Not even to be slit still alive for my diamond. But then Marie said, "I don't think it much matters anyway. I don't think anyone's going to be able to stop her now that she's found the way."

And as I spread some of my polythene further on the grass, for Maude to kneel on, I breathed more easier. And we helped her down before I gave her a trowel for her own.

"Make just a hole almost like this deep," I said to her. "Then we'll put a blue flower in."

And she started to dig very slow, lifting just a tiny bit of earth on the tip of her trowel each time, less than you would even get on a spoon. But, very slowly, a shallow hole got made, and when she seemed to think it was enough she did a smile at me, and I took a flower out from the tray. Before we planted it although, I pushed my own trowel down deep into the hole, and took out about two times as more than she had done—with just one scoop. Then we put the flower and the rich soil that was all packed tightly around its root into the hole, and I let Maude fill in what was left of the hole and I packed it down.

Then, after that, we did it all again. First with a blue one, then a red one, then a blue one again. And while we were doing it Marie began to talk some, in the voice that I even hear in my dreams now, and that even makes most of the hurts in my stomach go away.

"Remember I told you about the flower I planted in school?" she said. "The one that wouldn't grow? Well, because I got so upset about that, my grandfather helped me to plant another one in his garden. And then whenever we visited him I couldn't wait to see how much it had grown. And it did grow. I think I even gave it a name when the flower came out."

"What name?" I asked as I watched Maude dig determinedly, knowing of how she was getting to be tired by then, and hoping she wouldn't say about it just yet, so that they could stay for just a bit more.

"I can't remember," Marie said. "But I remember I cried when it died in winter. I've held a grudge against winter ever since too. I suppose it must be worse for you, though, you must really hate what it does to all your work."

I was just finishing pushing the earth tight down at another flower, and I spied at Maude anxiously to see if she would begin to dig a new hole, or if she would decide that was enough for today. But she did begin with making another one, and I relaxed to have the length of time it would take us to put one more in.

73

"Not mostly," I said to Marie. "Cause when I've cleared the mess autumn makes, winter makes gardening mostly easier."

But then I thought for how, this year, if I was still to be here, the winter would only mean one thing—that it was too cold for Marie to bring Maude to the garden. And then I began to feel resentful of it already.

So I told Marie all of most things about the winter lady, and what her cure for it was. I told about the way she followed summer around and about how, too, it made her not grow old. And how she couldn't stop now, because of how she would have to age all at once, and be over three hundred years.

And like she always does do, Marie only laughed.

"I like that," she said. "And she still looks the same now as she did when she began?"

"Yes," I said. And Marie nodded, looking away from me, and lifting up her eyebrows. I was just about to tell her about the time I tried to trick the winter lady too, by picking up all of the leaves. But just then, as I finished pushing the soil round another flower, Maude put her trowel down on the grass beside her, and that meant the minutes I'd been holding onto had passed, and all much too fast again.

"Enough, Maude?" Marie said, and Maude nodded and reached out to her stick.

So we helped her up slowly, Marie and I, and as I folded the polythene up, the pains started coming all into my stomach again.

"Alright," Marie said, and Maude put her free hand on her arm, and I stole a quick spy to Marie's face—and felt my heart get tight.

"Well," she said, "that's you freed from us again—at least until tomorrow. Thanks for your patience again . . . sir." And when she said "sir" she did a laugh. "We don't even know your name yet," she said, and I looked down at the trowel I had in my hand and tried very hard to be quiet. I didn't want to lie by telling her the name I'd told to Frank and Elizabeth, and I knew if I wasn't especially careful I would just tell her my real one right then.

"Ever the elusive," she said and did a laugh again. "Well, if you don't tell us by tomorrow we'll just have to make one up for you."

And after Maude had lifted her hand very slightly from Marie's arm and waved the tops of her fingers to me, they both turned around. And I watched them making a slow and careful way back up the lawns to the hospital building.

That's my hardest part always now, from every day: to watch Maude and Marie climbing slowly back up to the hospital building again. But once they are gone, and once they've been gone for about half of an hour—or sometimes a full one—I begin to have more of a good feeling again. That kind of liking the garden that I said about before, and an appreciation for it. And I think back on all of everything Marie has said, and I spy on the pictures of her I've kept in my head, and before long I always get to looking forward to the next day again. Only hoping that my jewel doesn't choose to arrive before then.

It gets to seem strange when I think about it properly, strange to think of how the things I used to long to do, and to have, when my diamond came, haven't been able to excite me any at all these last few days. I can't even hardly believe that what I enjoy most, and what I would choose, out of all of everything, is to stand stupidly helping an old woman to pretend she's gardening, while her nurse stands beside her and talks some to me while we're doing it. If someone had told me about that before I wouldn't never have believed it, and I'd have believed much less about me trying to make my jewel not come, just so's that I can keep on by doing it some more. In fact, if I'd known before that I'd still be having anything to do with gardening by this time it would have hurt me terribly. And yet . . . that's how all of it is. Not only am I doing like I am, but also, too, it's what I would choose to do. Out of all of everything.

But I think maybe I know for why, although.

There was a story Nalda used to say sometimes, you see, that I never could get to like much, about this old man she used to know who lived under beneath a bridge and only had one leg. He was very poor, Nalda said, and sometimes he always used to try and catch a fish beneath the bridge, for to eat, but the water was very dirty and very still and always, too, he never caught one. And then it was that the only time he could get anything to eat was whenever a kind person saw him and brought him some things.

The main thing was, although, that he hated it in there beneath the bridge. He hated the dirty water and the muddy bank, and he even hated the bridge. And all he did on all the days was think about these places he'd like to get to. Like the ocean. And like a big city where they have all these lights at night. Or like a cathedral, and a beautiful garden with flowers of all colours and trees. That was all he thought about the whole time, and about how quickly he would go if only both his legs were there. And he was tortured each time by not being able to see them, these places, and always tormented by the sights of the bridge and the dirty water and the muddy bank.

But one night it was, while he was asleep, an old woman as dirty as all the water and even more poorer than the old man himself came in under the bridge to be out of the rain. And when it was that the old man awoke up into the morning she was still there. And right from then the old man only wanted to be there beneath the bridge. The dirty water and the muddy bank became to be more beautiful for him than even a cathedral or a crown that a king would wear. Or an ocean or a garden. And he asked the old woman for to stay. And that was all.

Always I would ask Nalda about how come he didn't want to see oceans or cathedrals anymore, and I didn't like the story at all. I never did ask for it, but sometimes she just used to tell it anyway.

"A moment will come when you'll understand it," she said all times. "And that will mean you've fallen in love, with your high heart. Many times you'll fall in love—but mostly with your low heart, and that can only ever be a destructive and harmful thing. Your high heart will only fall in love once, and when it does you'll know why the oceans or the cathedrals didn't matter."

And always I didn't understand about it any at all. But now I think I do. And so that's why.

And I think, if the passing of my diamond didn't mean also that I'll be free always of such danger, then I think I wouldn't even care about that either anymore.

13

There is one thing I know for sure although, and it's that Nalda was right when she said those things about the very other kind of love, the kind that can come from your low heart. And about how it can make people become harmful and such.

There was this other place I once worked in, you see, and it was a private garden where only me and one other man worked. Mostly it was the other man who was in charge, but sometimes he used to go off quite early in the afternoons, and leave me behind on my own, to do whatever things needed doing.

We didn't have a proper shed there, I remember. And, instead, all the tools and the cutting machine and such things were kept in a joined-on part of the house, just a small little room. And we had our own keys for the door into there, that man and me.

Anyway, the thing I'm saying about just now happened one afternoon when the other man had gone home early again. I was up there in the place where all of the things were kept—sharpening the blades on a shearing tool. The thing was although, there was another door in that storing place that went on into the rest of the house, which was always locked. We didn't either of us have a key for that door, and I had never before seen anyone ever use it. But on that afternoon, while I was sharpening up the shearing things, I was sure I heard it opening behind me. And then, suddenly, I felt a hand being laid down on each one of my shoulders.

It made me truly terrified, and when I turned around I saw it was the lady from the house. And even worse than that, the very first thing she did to begin with was take the blades I was sharpening from out of my hands, and that made me get even more afraid by thinking she must have gotten to know all about me, and she was going to cut me wide.

All she did do with the blades, although, was just put them down carefully on a shelf, and then it seemed that she had forgotten all about them. And, instead, she began to speak, only it was in a strange kind of voice that I hadn't never heard her talking with before. And I noticed too then that she was wearing only a kind of a nightgown, but not like the kind Nalda always used to wear, it wasn't any like that at all. It was all kind of thin and short instead.

"I'm glad your friend's already gone home for the day," she said. And then she said some too about how she'd seen me watching her sometimes, when I really should have been working. And that was true, because I had spied quite sometimes when she was around in the gardens, just because she was beautiful. But she didn't say anything wrong about it while she was talking, she only just said that she had seen me, in that same funny voice. And then she said that she had been watching me too.

"You're very shy," she said, "but that's alright." And then she came even closer to me, and her voice got even stranger.

"Come on," she kept on by saying. "Come on . . ." And she pushed her body all up against me, and she took one of my hands and put it under on her leg, near the top inside. Then she started by pulling my belt too, and she moved her head down from mine, down further, doing all kisses and things. But just then, as she moved down closer to my stomach, I jumped a bit and the edge of the old metal tray I keep strapped around my stomach to protect me, it whacked her hard on her forehead, and she made this terrible loud scream.

"What in the Christ was that," she shouted. "Aoww." But then she only started by coming back towards me again, and she said, "Come on, what is that? Let me see what you've got in there."

And all I could do was just push past her, and then run out of the door and away. And all the time I could hear her shouting out angry things behind me, and things about the man from the house and what he would do to me one time. And as soon as I'd escaped I had to move on quickly from that place too.

So from that afternoon, always, I've known what it was Nalda meant by saying about the low heart, and I've known that she was true about it too. And now, also, I know she was true about the high one. Only, the thing is, I have that kind of idea about what you're supposed to do when it's your low heart that it happens to, but I'm not quite sure about what you're supposed to do when it's with your high one.

So, still, that keeps me a bit confused just now.

Guess what happened the last time Maude and Marie came down into the garden although. What it was, just like Marie had said on the day before, they'd made up a new name for me. And they told me about it.

I was tying some sapling trees to sticks to help them grow on that day, and I didn't even see Maude and Marie coming down the lawns. But the first thing Marie said when they reached close to me was, "We've got one . . ."

And I got quite a surprise, and turned around fast, and Marie laughed when I did that.

"I told you, Maude," she said. "Isn't it just perfect?"

But I didn't know what she was talking of right then, because I'd forgotten all about what she'd said on the day before. So I asked her what was perfect.

"The name we've picked for you," she said.

And when I'd remembered I asked her of what it was.

"Well . . ." she said, "because you're so elusive, and so easily startled—and because of that rusty beard, and all that rusty hair—we've decided you're just like a fox. You even have your own little lair down here. So we're going to call you Reynard, unless you change your mind, of course, and tell us your real name."

And to stop myself from just saying my real name right out I asked her what Reynard was.

"He's a famous fox," she said. "Haven't you heard of him?"

I shook my head.

"Alright then," she said. "Will we call you that?"

And I said they could.

I hadn't never thought, before, that I was anything like a fox although. In fact, I hadn't thought I was like anything much at all to other people. Not since Nalda. I mostly only thought they would think I was not like them. And strange. And that was all.

But when I told Frank and Elizabeth about what Marie had decided to call me, on that night, Frank asked me of what it meant. And when I told them about how it was a fox and about how Marie said I remembered her of one they both laughed, and they said it was kind of true.

"You always look a bit as if you're ready to run off at any moment," Frank said.

"And the colour of your hair too . . ." Elizabeth said, and they both laughed some more.

Mostly, the thing was, I only told them about all of it so's as it meant I could talk about Marie for a while, and even that's the reason for why I said about it here just now too. Because I didn't ever mean to say anything in here about what I look like, in case it could put me in danger—with everything you know about me now. But I'm still quite safe and hidden I think. Anyway, even though I only said about it to Frank and Elizabeth so's as to be talking about Marie, a good thing has come out from it too. As well. And what it is, they always call me by that name now too: Reynard. Instead of the one I made up for them. And that makes me feel much better, because, since they turned into being my friends, it made me feel like I was telling a lie every time they said that old one, and I didn't like that. So now it's better, and that's the good thing.

That night, we studied horses for the next day's races, Frank and me, once I had said all about that stuff. And I chose out only the horses with the high odds numbers, like I always do now.

The thing is, you see, when I went up to that little room on the evening after Frank had taken me on our trip to the betting place, it turned out that two of the horses I picked had won. Two of the ones with the high odds numbers. I didn't win any money of course, because of how all your horses have to win. But Frank decided then that maybe I have a lucky streak, and he said did I mind if he copied the horses I picked to put on his list, for the next while. Just the horses I pick with the high odds numbers although, because he already is quite lucky with his low number horses he says. And he thinks our two lucks might all add up together to make a winning.

So what we do now, at nights, I just choose the horses with the high odds numbers and Frank adds them to his list. And I don't make a list for my own anymore. I told Frank the reason for that was because of how I couldn't really afford it, but like you know that's not the one for true. I thought it might upset Frank by some too when I stopped doing it at first, but it didn't. All he did was make a wink and say, "I understand. To each his own."

And now I can even enjoy by picking the horses much more, just because I don't have to get worried in case they might win.

So that's what we did after I had told them all about Marie's new name for me, Frank and I, we picked our horses out in that way. And each time Frank or Elizabeth spoke to me they called me by that name, Mr. Reynard, and I enjoyed it. I enjoyed it just because it was something Marie had made up and because each time they said it it made me think of her, and even made me feel that a little tiny piece of her was right there with us.

And then I felt just exactly like the old man under in beneath the bridge, and I didn't want to be anywhere else in the whole world.

14

*M*arie and Maud didn't come down into the garden for another four whole days after they had first given me my new name, and the reason for that was because of how it began to rain without stopping. And even though Marie had said before that it would take a lot to keep Maude from the garden now that she had found the way, this rain was a lot. And it was enough.

It was even a lot for me, and I had to wear all of these special water-proof clothes on top, and work on things that were over by the wall on the other side of the garden from my own little quarters, where it was most sheltered.

I worked there with the rain driving into my eyes and running down on my face, thinking always and over on the collection of things I keep in my head now, of things Marie has said—and ways she's looked— when she's been down in the gardens in the afternoons. It almost saved me from growing too angry at the rain for making them stay away, do-ing like that. But as it went on and on I did begin to get some upset, without being able to help it anymore. And then I got to remembering how it used to be when I had to work with Nalda on the wet days, and how that had been.

Sometimes, you see, I had very bad tempers with Nalda on the wet days, and on the cold days too. And always, on the times when it had been wet for a few days in a line, the very first thing I would do when-ever Nalda shook me awake in the mornings would be to pull down the cloth that hung over the tiny window beside my bed. And if the rain was all still there I would crawl back down deep into my blanket and say I wasn't going. And then Nalda would have to lift me out and dress me all up in my working clothes while I stood just as tight and as unassisting as I could make myself to be.

Once I was dressed, always, I would ask her over and again to just let me stay, but she wouldn't never leave me by my own. Probably because of my valuables inside, it was. And I would have a temper through all the day then, and spend most of it by sheltering beneath a tree wherever we were working, which would never really shelter me properly. And every time when Nalda came across to try and ask me to do something, or even to just tickle me under the chin to try and make me do a laugh I would look on and away from her and make myself as stiff as I could.

And if it was the times when I was a little bit older I would wish of how she would just let me start going to school. Where I could be dry.

The thing is although, it hasn't been for years that the rain has made me feel almost that same way. All angry at it and in a temper. For a long time now lots of days of rain in a line is just another thing of gardening that I've learned to put up with, while I look on towards my jewel. But because of how, this time, it kept Maude and Marie away it got me to feeling almost all that way again. And it even got to be that, whenever I woke up on each morning, the first thing I did was wobble across and pull my curtain to the side, and whenever I saw all the rain was still there I even went back inside my bed for a while, and got a bad mood.

All except for this morning. Because this morning, when I pulled my curtain across, it was the sun that was shining, and all of the rain had gone. And I felt almost like when the rain used to end on those other times.

Whenever the day came when I pulled the cloth down to see the sun, I would jump out of bed all quick and fast, and I would dress myself up in my working clothes all hurried. I would do a smile at Nalda all day long and keep on by getting in her way while we were working, just because of how I wanted to be helping so much. And this morning I had a feeling that remembered me about all of that, and which was in some way even kind of the same.

Even better for me, although, was that I didn't even have to use my can any, which meant my jewel couldn't be there to steal away the day from me before it had started. And I just lay around in my quarters for a little while, until it was time for me to get all washed. And then I went eagerly out into the garden.

All my appreciating, and my fascinations, all of the things that had come into the garden with Marie and gone away out again with the rain, were back into place in the sun. Unlocking the shed doors even made me feel happy, not like on yesterday when I got all hateful at the tools and the work I was going to have to do with them. They seemed like they were even kind of friends to me today.

When I got back to the outside, too, it was true that all the rain had made the garden have an especial burst of life, like always it does do. All of the flowers were more colourful by some, and there were still drops of water hanging on them too, which made them glisten and shine. Just like the leaves of all the trees, and even a web that a spider had made between two stems.

So all morning I worked well and good, with an excited feeling in my stomach to wait for Maude and Marie. And I looked up at the sun over and again, watching it slowly going across the sky, and telling it to hurry for to reach halfway. Sometimes I looked up too soon after my last time and it hadn't hardly moved any at all, and I got to be impatient. But it did move slowly towards halfway, and my excitement got to be more and more, and I worked even more well and better, and the garden looked even more good as the sun came into more and more of it. And, at last, I saw a nurse wheeling old Will out in his chair, and after that I saw Marie helping some more people to the benches, and while I watched her moving around and then sitting down, I knew that it wouldn't be all so very long until her and Maude would be down beside me, with Marie talking.

I didn't let her see that I was looking at her any although, or I tried not to anyway. Just I looked up every little while, from at the very bottom of the garden, cautiously—to make sure and be certain that she wasn't spying at me before I looked at her. And then, when I was sure she was looking to another place, I would look up fully and watch her moving, and watch her smiling.

But one time when I did look up although, when I wasn't even looking up fully yet and still just checking, I could see that she was spying down to me. And as soon as I looked up even a tiny bit she did a wave to me, and then got up from off the bench. And when I looked up from my work the next time I saw that she was coming down the lawns towards me, already, but just on her own although.

"Good day, Mr. Reynard," she said in a pretend voice and did a laugh. "I'll bet this sun had you worried when you first saw it this morning."

I didn't know what she meant any, but I made a guess that it must be something to do with foxes, and I did a smile. Then I looked back down to my work.

"I've got some good news for you, though," Marie said, and that made me look back up again. "You can work on without interruptions today. And from now on, in fact, rain, sun, or whatever. Maude was discharged this morning, so you're a free man. No more having to put up with her getting in your way . . . and no more having to listen to me rattling on at you while she's doing it."

And she did a smile then, Marie, and I tried my best to do one back, but I don't really think it worked.

"I just thought I'd let you know," she said. "So's you can relax, and not keep wondering when we're coming down to annoy you." And then she turned around and walked back up the lawns, much faster than whenever Maude had been with her, and I dropped my hoeing tool onto the grass and went to sit in the sheds for a little while, in case anyone might see any of the tears I could feel coming down on my cheeks. And when I got in there I looked in my pocket for a handkerchief, but when I pulled out what I thought was it I found it was only the crumpled head from the flower I'd broke, that morning I'd thought Maude wouldn't come down because of some rain. And I dropped that down onto the floor, and ground it in with my foot, until all of the petals were torn and spoiled.

And I didn't go back outside until all of the benches were empty and clear.

15

I finished up with working very early that day. Or with just muddling around pretending I was working really. Anyway, I gave up on it earlier than I'm usually supposed to, and locked the tools I'd been pretending to use away in the shed. Then I went into my little quarters and just lay down on my bed, all in misery.

I got to be quite hungry while I was lying there too, but I didn't make anything to eat. All I did was just lie there and look up at the roof, waiting for it to be time for me to go and see Frank and Elizabeth, hoping that would cheer me up some amount.

The thing was although, when it was almost getting time to go there, and I was trying to tidy my hair with a brush, there was this knock on my door—on the door of my little quarters—and it made me even jump. I thought too that it could only be someone who had got to know all about me, coming for me at last, and I didn't even think I cared. Just that it wouldn't hurt too much or many. And I took in a big breath and opened the door very slowly, looking out from the crack it made, and growing warm while I waited to see who it was.

When I had the door opened enough I still didn't recognise the person who was out there although. Not from anywhere before. Then I got another fright, because she said, "Hello, Mr. Reynard," in this funny and pretend voice I had heard before, and I could suddenly see it was Marie—without her nurses clothes although. And without her hat too.

"How are you?" she said in more of her proper voice then. And when I pulled the door wider open I saw that she was carrying these two white bags, which she lifted up a bit to show me.

And then she came inside.

I'd had dreams in the past weeks, dreams while I was asleep and also dreams while I was awake sometimes too, which had made Marie be inside of my own little quarters, sitting talking on my own spare chair. And sometimes when I'd been alone there in mornings or at lunch times I'd even tried to imagine her there, in my chair that was always empty. I hadn't never thought that she ever would come into my little place although. Or not so soon anyway. But while she was there inside it didn't all seem so unusual. It didn't feel like so unreal as I would have expected it to do.

The first thing she did inside was to ask me if I was hungry, and when I said I was she said that was good.

"I was hoping you wouldn't have eaten yet," she told to me, and then she put her white bags on my table and took these silver containers out from inside, with cardboard tops on.

"Have you got some plates?" she asked. "And some forks and things?" And while I got all of that she sat down into my spare chair.

"Okay," she said, and forked the stuff out from the containers onto my plates. "That's it, just about ready. Come and get some." So I pulled my own chair towards the table and she pushed one of the plates over to in front of me.

"What is it?" I asked, and she did a smile.

"Chicken," she said. "The only thing for a fox." And then she laughed some. "I didn't catch it live like you might have done," she said. "But I hope that won't spoil it for you."

I ate a piece and it tasted good. Not like it usually does when I have chicken myself, because of how it had this kind of sauce on top. But I still liked it although. And as I took some more Marie opened up this bottle with wine inside, and she poured some of that out into glasses for us. Then she picked up her own fork and ate some from her own chicken, and while she did she looked all around at my own room, slowly.

"So . . ." she said after a little while, in her pretend voice. "So this is Mr. Reynard's little lair," and she did another smile at me, then went back to her proper kind of speaking. "I hope you don't mind me coming here like this," she said. "Or bringing all of this food and everything. But I just thought it would be a shame if we didn't see each other anymore, because of Maude going home."

And my heart went all crazy at that bit. I even felt like jumping up or doing a dance. But I didn't although. I only just took some more from my food and watched Marie quietly.

"I'll bet you thought," she said, lifting her eyes up towards the roof, "I'll bet when I told you Maude had gone home, you thought, 'Ah, thank Christ. No more of her getting in the way while I'm working, and no more of having to listen to that nurse rattling on at the same time. Prying and questioning all the time.'

"But you don't get rid of me that easily," she said, in her pretend voice again, laughing too. "And besides, I would miss hearing all of your crazy stories. So what do you say?"

I was drinking out from my glass although, and my mouth was filled up with chicken at the same time too, so I couldn't answer straight away.

"Hmmm," Marie said. "Not much, apparently." And she waited while I swallowed and chewed and then she said, "Would you like for us still to talk sometimes, even though Maude's gone?"

And I nodded.

"Good," she said. "Good." And just later, even although neither of us had said anything, and nothing had happened, she laughed some. And then she said, "As expansive as ever."

And I guessed that must just mean something to do with a fox too, and I did a smile on her.

It wasn't until we had finished eating although, and I was washing up our plates and things while Marie made them dry, that I remembered about Elizabeth and Frank. It wasn't until then that I remembered I was supposed to be up there helping Frank out with his horses, and all things.

I told Marie about that then, and I asked her if she wanted to come up there along with me too. But she had to go by then. She walked up the lawns with me although, and when we got to the top she said she would see me again on the next day. And then I went inside, back out of misery, and all in a happiness again.

Marie did a wave down to me the next day, when all of the nurses were bringing all of the patients out onto the benches. And then, after that, when they had took them all back inside and Marie had a short break for a while, she came down into the garden to talk to me some.

The first thing she did when she came down, although, was to lift one of my tools from out of the grass and to get in my way with it while I was working, pretending like she was Maude. Then she laughed and put it down again, and sat down on the grass beside it.

"Hello," I said, and still did some work a little bit.

"Hello, Mr. Reynard," Marie said. She had asked me if I'd been in time to help Frank pick his horses, and I'd explained to her about how I pick the long odds ones and he picks the shorts. And I told her that he'd already done his but left me mine to do, then she told me all about this thing she said she's been thinking about.

"I work here at nights as well as days sometimes," she said. "Or instead of days I mean. But a little while ago, when I looked out from one of the windows at night time, do you know what I saw in the dim lights?"

"No," I said, and she said it was a fox.

"I'm sure it was a fox," she said. "And I've watched out for it since then, and I've seen it once more at night and once in the very early morning. So," she said, "I've seen it in the garden, and I've seen you in the garden, but . . . and this is the important part . . . I've never seen both of you in the garden at the same time." And then she laughed and

91

said what she thought, what she'd decided, was that sometimes—in secret—I changed from being a man into being a fox, and then prowled around.

"That's what you're hiding," she said. "Isn't it? Am I right? That would just about explain things."

I put the tool I was using down on the grass and picked up the one Marie had been playing at Maude with instead, then I continued on with my work and Marie said, "I've decided, too, that what causes you to change is chicken, eating chicken. And that's why you had to rush off in such a hurry last night. It was nothing to do with Frank or Elizabeth, was it? It was really because you were just about to turn. Am I right? Isn't that the case, Mr. Reynard?"

And then we both mostly just laughed and giggled until it was time for Marie to get back to work.

She got up from the grass then, and said that she would see me again on the next day. But just before she began to walk up the lawns she said another one of those things, another one of those things that always take me by surprise and suddenly makes me think that she knows me all—just until I realise otherwise.

It was when she asked me once more if she had guessed correctly, and if her thing about the fox was true. And I couldn't think of a funny thing to say back, so I only just did a smile. And then she said, in a pretend voice like a villain, "Well, you might think you're safe at the moment, but be warned—I will bring out the secret thing that's inside of you. In time, my friend."

And it wasn't until she turned that I realised it wasn't my diamond she meant.

There's a funny thing about it although, and I'll tell you what. When I did think it was my jewel she meant, I was just as surprised as I always am to think of how she could possibly know. But the main thing was this; I didn't feel nearly as much afraid as I had on the other times. And more than that too, I think I even wanted her to know.

When I went up to see Frank and Elizabeth that night I told them all about what Marie had said about me sometimes turning into a real fox, just because it meant I could talk about her again. And it made me happy too that they both liked to hear about it, and it made me happy just because it was Marie's story.

"I didn't know we had a fox in the garden though," Elizabeth said when I had finished. "Do they come this close to the city?"

"There sits the proof beside you," Frank told her, doing a nod at me, and they laughed some.

"But seriously," Elizabeth said to me, "have you ever seen it down there?"

"Only when he's gone to lap from the fish pool and caught a glimpse of his own reflection in the moonlight," Frank said, looking up from his horse lists again.

I told Elizabeth that I never had, although, and that I'd never seen any signs of it in the soil or on the grass or anything.

"I think she only just pretends," I said, to try and get everyone by talking about Marie again. And it worked too.

"She has a crooked imagination, Marie," Elizabeth said. "She doesn't always pay quite as much attention to her work as she should do, but I like her. I get myself into trouble sometimes, covering up when it's her that should be in trouble."

"I like her too," Frank said and made a strange grin. "For sure."

And Elizabeth slapped his hair on the back and tutted.

"Come on, Frank," she said, "you could be her grandfather."

"Maybe so," Frank said, "but they often go for rich old men, these younger girls." And he did a wink at me and made his strange grin again.

"But you're not rich," Elizabeth said to him.

"Not yet, not yet. But it's only a matter of time. Especially now that I have this man stroke fox to help me, with his uncanny intuition for the animal ways. Come and look at this here," he said to me, and opened the newspaper that was on the table. "Take a look at this right here."

It was a picture of a man inside, holding up a big piece of cardboard with lots of words written on. And a money sign and numbers.

"Two hundred thousand pounds," Frank said to me. "Two days ago he was delivering letters, and after today he'll never have to work again. It makes you think, doesn't it?"

"It makes us think you're a dirty old man," Elizabeth laughed, and I asked Frank if it had been from horses that the man had won. It hadn't been although, it had been on another kind of competition that Frank explained to me, but I didn't really understand. Mostly because of how I wasn't listening so much. All I really wanted to hear was Elizabeth talking about Marie again, only I couldn't think of any more ways to get her to do it after that. Not except for just asking her, and I thought that might give my secret about Marie away.

So all I just did instead was help Frank choose his horses, and then we all watched at the TV for some time. And afterwards, back in my little room, I sat up by my window for a long while, watching out for the fox that didn't come. And I felt good just to be watching for it anyway, just because it was something to do with Marie. And the only reason I was disappointed when it didn't come was because I'd wanted to tell her the next day that I'd seen it.

But on the afternoon that followed, Marie told me about the plan she had made for how we could get to see it, or for how she could get to see it at least.

"All it needs," she said, "is for me to force-feed you some chicken again, and then keep you under close observation until the change takes place."

She said of it out in the garden, just after old Will and the others had all gone back to inside. And it still even made me laugh some when she brought another kind of chicken to my little quarters in the evening.

"It's nuggets in bread crumbs this time," she said, when she put her white bags down on my table. "And there are some chips in there too, just for the sake of variety."

Then, while I was bringing out all the plates and things, she took a camera out from in her pocket and put that on the table too, and I asked her what it was for.

"To record the changes," she said. "To show to you afterwards."

And I could see her trying not to let her face start laughing, and to keep it being straight.

"Alright," I said. And I tried to keep mine like that too, even when we had started eating.

Sometimes, although, when Marie would lean first one way and then the other—with her mouth full of food—to check my face from all sides for any changes, I wouldn't be able to stop it so much. And I would laugh some.

"Do you feel any different inside yet?" she asked me just after I had finished my plate, and I did a smile and shook my head. But I was lying although.

I didn't feel any different from having ate the chicken, and I certainly didn't feel to be any more like I was a fox-man. But I did feel different inside just because Marie was there. Sitting on my spare chair again.

"Well, it shouldn't be long now," Marie said, and she picked up her camera and turned some bits on it. "Just to be ready," she said.

But when it got close to being time for me to go up and help Frank with his horses, I was still just me. And Marie said it would be necessary for her to accompany me all the way there, to the door, just to make sure that was really where I went, and where I went straight away.

"I'll explain all about your condition to Elizabeth and Frank," she said. "And then they can keep an eye on you for the rest of the evening. And I'll leave my camera with them too, for them to record anything that might happen."

So we walked up the lawns, and on the way there I told Marie of how

I had already explained to Elizabeth and Frank about what it was she thought.

"All the better then," she said. "That means I'll only have to let them know you've had some chicken, and tell them to be sure and keep an eye on you."

And we walked for the rest of the way with our faces made to be straight, and Marie taking a study at my face sometimes and again, to check me for changes.

We both began to laugh all loud just after we passed through the swinging doors into the narrowest corridor although. Marie started first, and that broke up my straight face and made me by getting started. And then my laughing made Marie laugh more, and then that made me laugh more again too. And by the time we reached the door to the room Elizabeth had already came out to see what the noise was of, and when she saw it was us she started to laugh a bit too.

"Come in," she said. "Come in and spread some of that around in here."

So we went in, and we got to be quieter after we had sat down.

"Frank's been a little bit glum this evening," Elizabeth said, while she poured some glasses of port for us. "So it's good to see some smiles at last."

She put my glass down in front of me, and then she reached across and handed Marie's to her.

"There you go . . ." she said, and when she had put the bottle back on its shelf she sat down in front of her own drink.

"So what brings you here, Marie?" she asked, and Marie put her camera away into her pocket and blushed some.

"Well . . ." she said, and she looked at me. Then she looked over to Elizabeth and blushed again.

"She made me eat some nuggets of chicken," I said. "And she came up here to make sure I didn't be into a fox on my way up. And to ask you to watch any changes from me afterwards."

Elizabeth laughed too then, and even Frank—who really was looking quite unhappy—even he smiled some.

"Well, you must stay awhile and help us watch him too," Elizabeth said to Marie. "It would be a terrible shame to miss it all, wouldn't it, Frank?"

And when Frank looked up I got out from in my chair, and I went over to help him with the business of his horses.

16

When I sat down beside Frank I knew he had been working on his list for a time already. I can tell that now because of certain things. First of all, his little short pen, which he gets a new one of every day from the betting place, that gets chewed away down from the top. And then, too, the letters on the page which say about the horses and about their odds numbers—they all begin to wear away from how many times Frank's finger has run up and down on them.

But the thing was, even although everything was already like that, I could see as soon as I sat down that his betting slip was still completely blank.

He kept on by running his finger up and down on his list too, while I got to studying my own, but it was easy to know he wasn't really concentrating on it. And he did look just as glum as Elizabeth had said about. So all I did, I just went on by picking out my own horses, because I didn't know of what kind of things to say to him about. And when I had written them down I passed the piece of paper to Frank like I always do, but he didn't even ask me anything about their odds numbers this time, so's he could work out his sum. All he did was just write them on his own slip, and then go back to running his finger up and down again.

"Haven't you choosed any low ones yet?" I asked him then, and he shook his head.

"Not yet," he said, and did a sigh. And afterwards he made this kind of a smile that looked all tired. "The faith is weak tonight," he said, and put his chewed pen down. "It happens sometimes. It happens every now and again. And each time it does, I'm just a little bit older than I was the time before. And I realise that if it doesn't pay off soon then when life finally does come around, I might not have so very much time left to enjoy it. And to make use of it all."

Elizabeth and Marie had been talking away to each other for the whole time I had been doing the choosing with Frank, and they were still talking by then too. So what I decided to do, because Marie wasn't listening in—and that meant it couldn't bore her any—was I began to tell Frank all about the winter lady, and about what she used to do. But just after I had begun with it, Elizabeth and Marie finished up with what they'd been saying, and then they started listening in too.

I didn't hear Marie doing any groans or yawns or anything although, so I just carried on along with it, getting excited like I sometimes do up there. And I even added in some things I just remembered about other things while I was going, and I ended up by getting myself a bit confused, before I remembered what I was saying of again. And then I told Frank that he didn't have to be so unhappy about things.

"Because you can do just like that," I said. "Like the winter lady, when you win. And then you won't have to get any older. And you won't run out of time."

I heard Marie doing a laugh then, and that made me know she still only thought it was a story I had made up. But I didn't mind of any, and it got Frank to laughing some too, along with her. Which was the main thing.

"You know," he said with a wink to me. "I might just try that. I'll certainly keep it right here in mind."

And slowly he drifted back to his list, but more attentively. And he chose his horses quite easily, then asked me for the odds numbers of mine so that he could add his sum.

There was a thing Elizabeth said, just after that, which made me feel good in a kind of special way again. She said, to both me and Marie, that we were as crazy as each other with our stories, with the stories we told. And Marie said then, " . . . That reminds me, there should be some signs of the beginnings of a change by now. Can you see anything yet, Mr. Asher?"

And Mr. Asher was Frank, and Frank peered to my face from the side and examined me closely, while I stared to the list of horses on the table.

"I believe . . ." Frank said at last. "I believe his ears are slightly more pointed than before. And they've moved up his head a bit too . . ."

And I covered them over with my hands to pretend I was hiding the changes from view.

We all played some games of cards together, once Frank was finished and satisfied with his list. And while we played they kept on by doing studies of me again and over, and sometimes I put my cards face down on the table, to cover my ears up again.

Whenever everyone else was all caught up in the game although, I did some secret studies of my own, and only at Marie. And always I flicked my eyes up from my cards only to spy quickly, and to look back down again before she or anyone else could see me. And each time I did it my heart lifted excited, and then stayed feeling warm inside while I was looking at my cards some more.

I watched how her head did a frown when she was thinking on what card to play down, and I watched how the way she held her cards made them curve out towards the centre. I even tried to hold mine that way so's they did the same, but when I did I only dropped mine, so I didn't try that again. And I went back to only watching her some.

I spied on the way her hair fell down on each side of her face when it wasn't tied up to be a nurse, and I spied at her eyelashes flicking while she stared at her cards and put them into an order.

And then, one time, while I was looking at her face for just too long, she looked up and saw me, and she did a smile.

I was too caught by surprise to do one back although, so instead I put my cards down on the table and covered up my ears again, and she laughed.

"I don't think they have changed though," she said. And Frank and Elizabeth both looked up from their cards, and I drew my hands away.

"I must have been wrong about the chicken," Marie said. "That can't be what brings the change about after all. It must be something else."

"A full moon!" Elizabeth said, and Frank nodded.

"That'll be it," Marie said. "Yes, that must be it. So we'll just have to wait for the next one." And she asked when that would be, but everyone didn't know. "It must be soon though," she said. "We'll just have to wait."

And then we went back to our cards, and we played on until it was time for Frank and Elizabeth to go home.

"I don't suppose there's much point in me staying around now either," Marie said, while Frank washed out our glasses and Elizabeth tidied some other things away. "Not since we know you won't change until the moon does." And after Frank had picked up his slip, and folded it away into the pocket on his shirt, we all of us left the little room together.

"I appreciated your help tonight," Frank said to me quietly, as I watched him locking the door. "I always do, of course. But tonight especially." And then we walked to the swing doors, where Marie was holding one of them open for us.

"You should come up more often in the evenings," Elizabeth said to her. "You certainly helped Mr. Reynard make Frank look a bit less glum—which isn't always the easiest thing in the world to do."

And Marie thanked her for the invitation, but she didn't say if she would come up again or not, which was what I really wanted to know.

There was a surprise waiting for us when we got out through the main doors although, and this is what it was:

Hanging up high over the top of the gardens, making them look all shining, was a perfectly full moon. And we all did a laugh when we saw it.

"Maybe you should keep an eye on him just a little bit longer," Elizabeth said to Marie, as she and Frank went off towards the gates. And Marie did a smile at me.

"I suppose I'd better do," she said. "Just for a little while."

And after we said "Good night" to Elizabeth and Frank, we stood for some moments and stared up to the moon.

"I really should be going too," Marie said. "But . . . I'll walk down as far as your little house with you, just to see what kind of effect this has on you now you're out in it. And then I'll go."

17

I walked just as slowly as I could going down the lawns, hanging onto the minutes like it used to be when Marie always brought Maude into the gardens, and wishing too that she didn't have to go soon, just like then.

But when we got down as far as the fish pool I saw the reflection of the moon lying on the water, and that reminded me of a story Nalda used to tell. So what I did, just to give me some more added minutes, I pointed at the floating moon and told the story to Marie, knowing she wouldn't go before the end.

It was about a river, the story. A river near where I used to live with Nalda, with this bridge that went high up over. And every time the moon was out you could see it sitting down there in the water, from up on top of the bridge.

"But if the moon was a full moon," Marie asked, when I had only just said about that, "did that see you dropping down onto all fours, and suddenly coming over all canine?"

"I don't change," I said, and I looked up to the real moon so's its light spread all over my face. "Look. It's all on me," I said, "but I don't change."

"I'm beginning to think that's the truth," Marie said. "I didn't want it to be, but I'm beginning to think it is."

So then I told her the rest of Nalda's story.

And what it was, it was about this man who was Nalda's friend one time. He lived in the same town as us, and what he always wanted to do, more than anything else in the whole world, was to throw his arms around the moon. So one night, when the moon was there in the river, he jumped off from that bridge. To try.

"But just when he did," I told Marie, "just when he got down into the water, a cloud passed across in the sky. And then he couldn't find the moon in there, to put his arms upon. And he drowned."

"Trying to put his arms around the moon?" Marie asked, and I nodded some. Then Marie made a smile, looking at the moon in the pond, and she said for me to try it. But I shook my head.

"There are no clouds tonight," Marie said. "You'd be alright." But I still shook my head, and just stared into the water to watch the dark back of one of the fish I could see. Then I looked to where both our shadows were close together on the grass beside the pool.

Because of how the moon was shining, and where it was shining from, it made our shadows be closer together than we were. And what I did, when I knew for sure that Marie wasn't looking at our shadows also, I moved my hand so that my shadow one moved too, and I made it just touch against Marie's shadow hand—even although our real hands were far and apart. Then, when Marie turned around towards me again, I sneaked my hand away. Quite quickly.

I thought too, then, that Marie would be turning to say it was time for her to go now, but she wasn't. That wasn't what she said. She said instead that, with the moon lying on the surface of the little pond, and with the white and gold fish swimming around beneath it and beneath the leaves which had fallen in on top, that bit of the garden reminded her of how she would imagine a Japanese place to be.

"Don't you think so?" she asked. "Isn't it a bit like that?"

But I said I didn't know, because I hadn't ever really imagined a Japanese place.

"Well, this is just about how I think it would be," Marie said. "Except everything would be a bit bigger—apart from the trees. The pond would be bigger, and the fish would be too, and even the reflection of the moon would be bigger. But the trees would be smaller, because a lot of trees in Japan are very small. Did you know that?"

I shook my head.

"Well, they are. They have very small trees there, very beautiful and very small."

"Have you been to there?" I asked her, and she said she hadn't, but that she always thought she would want to.

"Sometimes," she said, "when I'm truly tired of coming here day after day, and when I just get sick of looking at the corridors and all the wards, I really wish that's where I was. And then I get sad to think I'll probably never be able to afford to go, and I'll always be here."

And that was when I suddenly got excited. And because I was, and also because it was something to keep Marie there for some more, and also, too, because I somehow just wanted to anyway, I did my very most dangerous thing from ever. I said of how, one day, if she wanted, I could take her to there. Even for forever if she liked. And she did a laugh and said I probably had even less money than she did.

So then I told her of how it would be possible.

I said of everything: of my father; of the diamond itself; of how we had been trapped in that little room; and then of how he'd fed it to me. I got so excited that I even forgot to hang to the minutes as I was telling, and it all went past much faster than I'd wanted. Before I even knew it I was telling about my waiting, and it wasn't until then that I realised quite how I'd rushed, and how I'd let the moments run off.

"I think that's my favourite story of all the ones you've told me," Marie said when I'd got to being finished. And then I told her that just as soon as my diamond did come I would take her to that place, and she did a smile, and said she would look forward to it.

I could tell although, just as from ever before, that she didn't think it to be true and that she thought I was only weaving something for her again. But it didn't matter so much. It only mattered that she'd said she would look forward to it, and when my jewel did come she would get to know soon enough. And then we could go for real to that place.

But let me tell you about the most special thing from all now. Let me tell you about this.

Not long after I'd finished with my story Marie said she would have to go, and we were still standing beside the fish pool then, and I was still looking at our shadows on the grass sometimes. But when Marie began to move towards the lawns I looked up to see her properly, and this is what she did.

She lifted her hand, up from her side towards her mouth. And then she put her fingers in front of her lips and she kissed them. But just before she said of how she would see me again on the next day—and just before she turned away to go—she made her fingers flat beneath her mouth.

And I don't know if you'll even believe it or not, but the true thing is that before she left, she closed her eyes . . . and then she blew her kiss to me.

18

We made things be a different way around for a few nights after that, Marie and me. What it was—the change—instead of her coming always with our food in white bags in the evenings, instead of that I cooked extra whenever I made my own dinner. And then Marie always came to eat of that.

Ever since I'd told Marie the secret about my jewel although, I couldn't stop by telling her of all kinds of other things, even though I knew she thought I was only telling tales. And whenever she came down to have dinner at nights I just kept on by spilling things out.

I told her all about how we used to do the gardens when I was very young, and about the way Nalda put the spell on me to make me able to ask other people if they had any work for us to do. And I told her all about how Nalda looked, with her skirts and her rings, and the silk kind of scarf covering her hair.

And I even told her many things about our little van at the bottom of the road, and all about the sofa that sat outside.

She liked to hear of it all too, Marie. She always listened carefully, while we were eating our things, and she always asked lots of questions. And while she was asking, and while I was telling too, I always spied in secret upon her loops and on her arms, and on the lid tops of her eyes while they were looking down to her food.

Let me tell you now about a thing that happened a few times on; a few times on from when we first made things be like that, on one evening when we were both eating of some fish I had cooked.

I think Marie had asked me to say some more about Nalda, and I was telling of how it was with Nalda and me and Nalda's stories; of how it was when she was telling me of myself, and how I always asked for the best ones I liked over and again. And then I changed to saying some about how it was when the people always came around to try and make me come to school, and how Nalda used to make me hide. And even I said just a tiny bit about when Nalda began to shout, but that was an accident, it just slipped out. And I didn't want to say so much about that.

It was when I had finished with telling about all those things although, and when we had almost finished with eating of the fish I had made, that was when the thing happened I'm telling about just now.

Marie had just put her fork and her knife down together on her plate, and she had pulled some of her loops back behind her ear. And then she made her tongue go around her lips and smacked a loud noise.

"Delicious again," she said and did a smile. And then she put on a pretend voice to say, "I think I'll just go and powder my nose now." And she got up from out of my spare chair and went off towards my toilet room.

What I'd done for the first time ever, although, I'd forgotten to hide my can away in a secret place before she came down, and it was still hooked up to the toilet in there. And I didn't remember any about it until Marie had gone.

It was cleaned up and everything, and so were my fork and such—which were lying together with my magnifier glass up on top by the toilet. But I still felt quite embarrassed for Marie to see it all there. And also, too, I knew she wouldn't be able to use the toilet while it was still there, and that she would have to come back to get me to remove it. So I took our plates to the sink while I waited for her to come back, and I cursed on myself.

Marie looked kind of strange when she did come back, although. She was frowning some, and then, also, she was staring to me kind of like a question.

"Did . . . ?" she said, and pointed off some. Then she frowned some more. "Is that as a joke for me?" she asked, and I tried to make a smile for her. But she didn't do one back. Instead she still just frowned and stared at me. Then she came more into the room and turned the spare chair to face away from the table and towards the sink. And she sat down.

I wasn't quite sure what to do then, because of how she wasn't saying anything. She was only just sitting with her frown beneath her loops, sometimes looking like it wanted to turn into a laugh, if only I would say the right thing, and then getting to be even more of a frown. So I turned to the sink and put some water on. Then I dropped the plates and things in.

She did begin to speak when I stopped the water running, but only very quietly although, and without any at all of her pretend voices.

"I . . . You really believe all of those things you've told me," she said. "Don't you?" And when I turned around she was looking at me in this kind of way I had only ever seen Nalda do, sometimes. When she was very concerned. Like on this one time when I fell from a tree I'd climbed in one of our gardens, when I lay very still on my back on the ground for a while, waiting to see what would hurt. Or else from this other time when I was standing too close behind Nalda when she was digging, and she hit me on the head with the spade. Marie was looking at me with an expression like that—an expression like the one Nalda had when she dropped the spade and parted my hair with her hands. So I looked across to the door.

"I didn't think . . ." Marie said, still very quietly, and still with none of her pretend voices at all. "I didn't think for a minute . . . but I'm not wrong, am I? That tin and those other things, they're not just there to play a joke on me, are they? You really do believe what you told me, you believe it's all true, don't you?"

And I nodded. I did a smile again too, to see if it would make any difference yet, but it didn't. Marie's face just quickly looked like Nalda's did sometimes when she cried—when she cried and it was me who had hurt myself. Then she said, "Oh, Mr. Reynard . . ."

And got out from her chair to come towards me. And I had no idea about why, for any of it.

19

That was really all she said then, Marie, just "Oh, Mr. Reynard . . ." as if I'd hurt myself in a bad way. And while I stood by the sink, looking away towards the door, she kept coming closer to me all the time, until she was up beside me. And then she lifted one of my hands from my side, and gripped it between both of hers. And she bent her neck forwards and pressed all three of the hands against her forehead, without saying a word.

Sometimes, when I'd stood close to her in the gardens before, I'd trembled some. And I began to tremble like that again, only stronger. I don't think she could tell, because the hand she was holding was mostly okay, but all down from my neck, and in my legs too, they were very tight. And it was almost like I was afraid.

"I think it's time for me to help Frank now," I said, to have an excuse to move, and it came out in this strange voice that I hadn't really heard from me since the first times I went up to see Elizabeth and Frank. When I was still nervous of them and things.

She slowly loosened her grip when I said that although. She loosened it just enough for me to take my hand back, and she kept her own hands and her head in place. Then, after I had taken my hand away, she lifted her head up slow, without looking at me at all, and she turned back towards the table and looked in the opposite way from where I was.

I still didn't move much at first, I only just put the dish-washing rag down and kept on by still shaking some. And Marie stood still for a while too. But soon, she asked if she should come up with me tonight like usual, and I said "Yes."

"Well," she said, kind of in her pretend voice, with just a bit of the real one still there. "Maybe I'll wait and powder my nose up there instead."

And then we went up, really without saying anything all the way. I kept turning to spy at Marie as we climbed the lawns, to see if she was about to say something. But always she was just looking straight ahead, not smiling or anything. And I didn't know enough about the reason why to ask her any questions. So I just stayed by being silent, and tight to trembling.

That was the strangest of any nights I've ever spent with Elizabeth and Frank, that night. I did help Frank with his horses, like as usual. But it was mostly very different apart from that.

As soon as we both came into the little room Elizabeth and Frank looked at us in a different way, like as if they knew a thing had gone wrong. They didn't try to find out what it was although, or try to make us be any different or anything. They only just stayed quiet while I helped Frank with his list. And then, when he had done his sum, I saw Elizabeth looking to him for some minutes until she finally caught his eye. And she lifted her eyebrows and tapped her emptied-out glass on the table, until Frank quietly moved his chair back and did a small cough.

"I think," Elizabeth said, "I think Frank and I will go now, and give you both some time on your own." And Frank took their coats from their hooks, while Elizabeth did us a nice smile.

I thought she was going to say something else then too, because I saw her mouth opening like as if she was about to, but she didn't. She only just looked at me and Marie with a kind of concern, and then fixed up all the buttons on her coat.

"We'll see you both tomorrow," Frank said finally, and he lifted Elizabeth's bag from down on the floor beneath the coat hooks. And after they had gone, and after we had heard the sound of the doors in the corridor swinging closed, Marie looked at me without speaking or without smiling or without anything. And then she went across to the cupboard where the port is always kept.

Mostly, for all the time Elizabeth and Frank had been there and really since Marie had got up from my table to go to the toilet room, I had only been confused by everything. I hadn't been able to think out any words to say to her, mostly because I didn't know why she had become so strange over it all. And I had only been waiting for when she would talk some, to tell me what had made things be so very strange. So when she moved on her chair to face me I continued on by waiting. I didn't turn around to face her, I just kept my head stiff and my eyes straight, looking down to my drink on the table and only seeing her from my corners, and I waited on and on, till at last she said, "So . . . Mr. Reynard . . ."

And then, still from my corners, I saw her sitting up more straight, and I turned some so's I could look at her sometimes. And when I did she held a hand to me, for me to take. And after a little while I did, and we sat with our hands joined up, not looking at each other. And this time I didn't tremble so much.

"Tell me some things, Mr. Reynard," Marie said quietly then, as she lifted her glass with her other hand and leaned back. But I had no things to tell. I was still waiting for her to say about what had made things be so strange, and I had no ideas about what to say of any other things. So I just asked her, "Things about what?" And she said, "I don't know . . . Some more things about Nalda. Tell me about that."

And I asked her what kind of things.

"Well . . ." she said, "like . . . what age were you when she told you all about your father and about the diamond?"

"I was lots of ages," I said.

"So what age were you when she first told you about it?" Marie asked and I shrugged.

"I don't know then," she said. "Tell me other things instead. When . . . What age were you when Nalda first began to shout?"

"About eight years," I said. "Or nine." And I wished I hadn't never let slip out about that. I lifted my glass and gulped from some, and as I put it back down I hoped that would be enough about Nalda's shouting. But it wasn't although. When I leaned back Marie squeezed on my hand and she said to say more about that.

And, in the end, just because it was a tiny bit better than sitting there so quiet and confused, I said as much about it as I could remember.

20

At first, Nalda didn't shout very often. It was only just sometimes, and not for long either. So that's what I started off by telling Marie, and when I had she asked what Nalda shouted about. I couldn't remember so much about that although, not from then. She didn't shout much about whatever it was. And only ever in the van or around it outside.

But each time she did shout, it was worse by some than the time before. And it went on. And when I was ten years, by about that time, it was bad by then. She didn't ever shout at me, Nalda. She only just shouted. But when it got bad she didn't only shout in the van or around the van anymore, she shouted just about anywhere. And she shouted for a long time too.

Sometimes it was when we were doing work in someone's garden, or when we were walking the roads to or from there. Or sometimes, too, it was when Nalda was hanging our clothes out to dry. And even, sometimes, when we had been sitting in the van she would just throw the door open and go out onto the step to shout—up into the street that our little van was at the bottom of.

Marie moved closer to me in her chair when I said about that last thing, and she put her other hand on top of mine, so's she was holding it in both her hands. And because I could feel her spying so hard at the side of my face like that I turned around to see her some, and she said, "So all the things you've told me about living in that little van were really true? I . . . oh, I always thought all those things were only to weave a mystery. I've been away along on the wrong road, Mr. Reynard, from the very beginning . . ."

I waited then to see if she was going to bring her forehead down onto our hands like before, and I was glad when she didn't. All she did do was keep on by holding my hand in both of hers, and then she asked me to say some more about Nalda. So I told her all about the people who lived on our street, in the white houses, how they always came out onto their front steps when Nalda began to shout at first. And how some of them came down to our van to ask Nalda what had happened, and to see if she was alright. But the thing was, whenever the people got close it made her shout more. And if they reached out for her she threw her arms about to keep them away, until they all went back to their houses again.

"Weren't you ever frightened?" Marie asked me and I told her that I always was. But I told her too that it got so I could mostly tell when it was going to happen, and that made it be not so bad.

What it was . . . she would always look as if she was just about to cry. And maybe she would just be in the middle of talking, or even just watching some other people or something. But then, instead of tears that came out, it would be shouting instead. And after a while the people from the white houses didn't come down anymore when it was happening around the van. They just looked out through their windows and then closed them. And people who were out on the street, or in their gardens, they would either shout other things back at Nalda or else go inside their house until she'd stopped. And the extra thing was too, that after a while not many people on the street talked to us anymore, not even when Nalda was just fine. They would mostly look away at another thing whenever we passed them. And if there was more than one of them we sometimes heard them whispering a thing like, "That poor little boy . . ." Or some other kinds. But then Nalda would always do me a special smile and we would giggle. Because they didn't know how good we were on most days.

She always did keep on getting worse although. And after some more years she became afraid of people seeing her when she wasn't in her right way, and she took to just staying at the van most of the time, without ever going out.

By the time I was about fourteen years it was only ever me who went to work anymore. I had to get all the jobs, and I had to do them all on my own too. But people were kinder to me by then, once Nalda didn't come anymore. They always gave me things to do as if they wanted to help us, just so long as Nalda wasn't there to frighten them.

Mostly I had to do all our food by then too, and our washing and things. And Nalda didn't even like to tell her stories much anymore. She mostly just slept a lot, if she wasn't shouting. And then, one time, she pinned this telephone number up on the wall, beside the window, and she said that when she asked me—if she ever did—I was to go straight away to a phone and dial the number. And then I was to tell the people who answered where we lived, and I was to ask them to come and help her.

"You know," Marie interrupted in, when I was telling about that, "I even thought, before, that Nalda was just another invention of your own. I thought she was just one more detail you'd woven to hide yourself . . ."

And I told her of how I'd mostly known about that, but that I didn't mind so much. And she said she was sorry for thinking that, and then asked me if I'd ever had to call the number.

"I didn't never want to," I said, and I told her of these dreams I'd sometimes had from that time, where I'd had to make the call. And I told of how they'd always made me wake up by weeping, and of how I'd always kept on weeping until I saw Nalda still lying across from me on her own bunk.

Sometimes although, at that time, when Nalda was feeling mostly okay and well, she would speak about how good things would be for me after I had called that number. She told me how they would find someone to look after me who knew how to do it properly, and not in the bad way she had done. And she told all about the things I would have, and about the proper places I would live in. But I didn't never want to hear about it, and I only ever asked if we couldn't just take the number down. Take it down and throw it away. Because I didn't never want that we should need it.

But we did need it although. One day, when I was just nearly sixteen years, I came home and Nalda was sitting on the stool beside our stove, with something all running down her face. I'd brought her some flowers home that she liked to have, but when I held them out she didn't take them. It didn't even seem like she could see them. And when I got closer I saw that—very carefully—she was scratching her face with her long sharp nails, and I saw that the stuff on her face was blood.

It was a time and more before she finally saw me standing there, but when she did she looked at me almost as if she was saying sorry. And she continued on by scratching, away in deep, almost as carefully as she used to put her special cream on. And then she said, "Phone now," very calmly, without being in a panic. And I ran out to do it.

Her hands were shaking so much when I got back that she couldn't scratch with them anymore, and when she saw me looking at them she sat on top of them instead. Some blood was dripping down from her chin onto her shirt, but it was only her hands that shook; the rest of her body was quite still. And then she started to cry, and that made her hands stop too.

"You'll be alright," she said to me then, and she came closer to cuddle against me, and soon it got that I was crying too, and her blood was all on my face and on my clothes.

"Things are going to be much better for you from now on," she said. "I promise." And then she said of how sorry she was. About things.

We were still stuck together like that when the people came, and I think they thought we were both hurt to begin with. But when they had worked out it was only Nalda they helped her very slowly outside, to this van they had waiting there. And while they were doing that I sneaked away to spy from behind a wall, just so's as I wouldn't have to talk to them.

And for a little while they tried to find me, after Nalda was inside the van. But I was hidden well, and they couldn't. And eventually they had to just drive away.

And once I was sure they were really gone, and they hadn't left anyone else behind to watch for me, I came out and went back inside. And from then on I didn't never see Nalda again.

21

So I told Marie all about those things, and now she really does believe Nalda to be true. And all the other things that used to make her laugh, and make her think I was just weaving—like our little van, and me not going to school—she believes all about them now too. But it's still the same with Nalda's stories, she still thinks they're just made up. Except, now, instead of thinking I made them up for her, she's changed her mind to thinking it was Nalda who made them up herself. For me.

That was even what made things be so strange that night, I've found out, when she saw my can still hooked up in my toilet room. And that was what made her look at me as if I'd hurt myself too. It was because she knew then that I really believed in my jewel, and because she thinks it isn't true.

The thing is although, I suppose I should be glad for her not believing about it, because of how it keeps me safe. But it's somehow not like that, and it even makes me unhappy. Especially when she tries to convince me that Nalda just weaved it all for me. That makes me the unhappiest of all. Because then I know just how untrue she thinks it all to be.

So when it was lunch time today, and Marie had some time free, I did a very special thing. We went inside my little quarters, and I did a thing I had never done for anyone else before. I showed her the book I keep my clippings pasted into, that no one else has ever seen.

Always, wherever I am, I keep my book hidden in a special place—in case anyone should find it and work a few things out for themselves.

So, for all the time I've been here, I've kept it hidden beneath the seat of my own chair, which comes off and which there's a big space beneath.

When Marie came into my room although, the very first thing she did was sit down on that very chair, and I had to tell her to move some.

"That's where I keep it hidden," I said, and then I took a spoon out and levered the top off.

It looks old now on the covers, my book. And inside, too, a lot of my clippings look very old. A couple of them have even come to be unstuck and always drop out whenever I open the book. And a few more have begun to curl up from the sides, where I didn't never glue them down properly to begin with. I always mean to stick those ones back down properly when I'm putting something else into the book, but I never do. I always end up by just leaving them again.

So I put the book down carefully on the table when I'd lifted it out, and Marie pulled her own seat in closer while I fixed the top back onto mine. Then I sat down and turned through some of the pages while she watched.

"These first things," I said, still turning, "all these are bits I cut from newspapers and books I found, saying things about my diamond, and where different people think it is now. But these big ones, these are some pages I found that tell the whole history of my diamond— from the first time it was found, right up to when it was taken away. It tells you even of all kings that owned it from each other, and like that."

And I left the book opened to the beginning of those pages for her, and then pushed it across.

"I found them in a book in a library one time," I said to her. "A book about all kinds of famous diamonds, and I got all excited looking to see if mine was in it, and when I saw it was I went behind some shelves and tore out the pages."

Marie looked up from what she'd already begun to read then and did me a smile, but she didn't stop long enough to say anything. She just dropped her eyes straight down again and went right back to reading, and I got up from my chair and went to look from the window for a while.

I watched out at the garden for quite a time, just to give Marie some peace to read in. And after that I came to stand by her chair, to look at the book along with her. And when she had finished with the big pages, and moved onto all the little bits of the ones I had clipped, I said, "No one in any of them, not anyone knows where the jewel is."

"So it seems," Marie said.

"There are more on the other pages too," I told her, and as she turned over I went back to my own chair again and just sat there quietly until she looked up from the pages, and put her mouth to one side.

"You see?" I said then. "They really are all from newspapers I cut, from all different times. And all the things are just like Nalda said, away from before."

Marie turned back to the first pages I'd shown her then, and slowly moved through till she came to the place where she'd finished again. But she wasn't reading anything this time, she was only just looking. And then she passed the book back across to me.

"Tell me about what you did after Nalda was first taken away," she said as I took it back and turned it around to face me. "What did you do then? Did you leave the town?"

"Not for a while," I said, and I looked through the pages in the book myself. "I just kept working in the gardens there like I had been, and still staying in the van there too. But when I came home one night I saw some people sitting down around the sofa outside, and I could recognise one from the doctors who came for Nalda. So I hid in a place until they went away again. And then, on that night, I got some of my things into my cloth bag and I left."

I closed my book up then and flattened its covers down, but I was kind of hurt, because of how Marie had only asked me that thing after reading it, and hadn't said anything else.

"But don't you believe about my jewel now?" I said to her, as I levered the top from my chair again with the spoon, and put the book back inside. "I told you it was real about it. And those parts in my book, they say the same."

"But that doesn't mean . . ." Marie said, and then she stopped. "I mean, the diamond you told me about is certainly a real diamond. But . . . I just think there are some things you've misunderstood."

And I just couldn't think of any more things to do or say to try and convince her then, so instead I only stared out towards the window and didn't say a single thing. Marie looked over to the window too when some bits of time had gone past without me still answering, and she asked me what had caught my attention out there. But I still didn't answer any. I only just kept on staring, and while I did I could feel her spying some at my face and after a while I looked down to my dinner things instead.

"Aren't you speaking to me anymore, Mr. Reynard?" she asked then, but I still didn't answer. So she put on a pretend voice which was supposed to sound like me and she said, "Did I do a thing to make you not want to say any more?" And when I only tipped my head for an answer and kept on by only staring at my plate, she asked me over and again to tell her what was wrong, what she had done. So, in the end, I did. I told her it was because she didn't like Nalda, and thought she was wrong. And thought she did wrong, and told me lies. That was all I said, only that. And when I had, I looked back to the window, and I could feel her spying at my face again.

"But that's not what I think at all," she said. "Not at all. I think Nalda was very clever, and very special too. It's . . ."

But I didn't wait until she had finished although. Before she had even got to the end of her sentence I broke in right on top, right over her words. And what I was saying was, "But how come if you like about Nalda, and how come if you don't think she did wrong and made lies, then . . . but you must although. You must still, if you still don't think about my jewel being true. You must . . ."

And I heard Marie laughing just a little bit when I had stopped. And I looked up at her then and she curved her hand around the handle of her fork, making it stand up straight by pushing it hard against the table. And then she rested her chin down on top of that hand, and stuck her bottom lip out just a bit while she was spying up at me like that.

"Well, why must I?" she said. "I think, honestly, that Nalda was probably very brilliant and very wise. That's the truth, Mr. Reynard."

"But you can't," I said, "because how come if . . ."

Only, this time, it was Marie's turn to break in over on top of my words, and to not wait until my sentence was finished.

"Well, the thing is," she said, "you were so young when Nalda told you all of the things she told you. And I don't believe she meant it all to be left like that, I believe she had a lot more planned for you, and that she meant to explain it all a lot more thoroughly to you the older you got. But then she got ill, and it all got confused. But I don't really think she meant any of those stories literally, Mr. Reynard. I don't think she meant them to mean just what they said. Do you see what I mean?"

But I just put the last piece from my plate into my mouth, and I didn't make any hurry to chew it away. I chewed just as slowly as I could in fact. And when I had chewed it all away, instead of answering, I lifted my glass and emptied that too. Then I just said, "No."

And I looked down to my fork and my knife, as I positioned them close together on my plate.

"Well, what I mean," I could hear Marie saying, "is that when Nalda said you had a jewel inside you, that probably wasn't exactly what she meant. Not literally. Probably . . ."

"Yes it was," I shouted out, and I surprised us both some. But I was just tired and sad, and upset that still she wouldn't believe about it. "That was really what she meant," I said more quietly, and when I looked up Marie was only looking concerned again. And that made me sadder too.

"But Mr. Reynard . . ." she said, "don't you know it's impossible for a jewel to still be there inside of you? Don't you know that?"

And that was when I stopped trying to make her see, and we just sat in quietness after that, until it was time for us both to go back to work.

123

22

Over the past few days now, I've gone back to eating in just the way I always used to do, and I've been thinking that I would give just anything at all if only my jewel could come right at this very time. I would even give the diamond itself away I think, if that's what I had to do. And it's all because of what I would like to be able to do one time when Marie starts off by saying, "But Mr. Reynard . . . Don't you see? Don't you know that it can't be in you?"

I want to be able to do a smile and say, "But I know it's not."

And then she would look all pleased, because of how she'd think she'd got me to believe her at last. And all her concerned looks would be gone, and she'd be happy and pleased. And then what I would do, I would put my hand very slowly into the pocket of my gardening coat, and I would hold my palm flat out with my jewel just sitting there, all cleaned. And I would say, "It no longer is inside me."

And then she would know. And then she wouldn't always say lies and things about Nalda anymore.

I did come up with one more thing I thought might help her to believe about it all, after she had gone away that day, and that was to tell her all about the way my stomach always hurts so badly sometimes. So when she came down on that evening I told her about that, and about the way I can feel my jewel moving around in there too. But it didn't make a difference. She only just looked sorry for me—on her face— when I had finished saying it. And that made me get so angry that I began with shouting again. And I shouted that it certainly was all true, and that she was stupid and wrong. And then I even felt like crying some.

But the thing was, Marie didn't shout back any. She looked as if she was going to, for some, and as if she was just as angry and upset as me. But she stayed silent for a bit of time, and then her face got clear of being like that. And instead she did a different kind of smile to me, and she started saying like, "Well, let me see if I can feel it, Mr. Reynard. Let me see."

And then she kept reaching out and taking her hand back, and making me feel like she would tickle me. And she kept laughing all at the same time too, until it became that I was laughing along some. And then she started by chasing after me, and I kept on by jumping back while she was saying, "Come on, let me try. Let me touch."

And on and again round the little room. But when she reached out one time she reached out just a bit too far. And her hand hit me, and it happened that it hit my protector. And all at once she stopped.

"What was that?" she asked, kind of as if she wasn't sure if she'd hit something or not.

"It was only just my protector," I said back, and she sat quietly down onto my spare chair.

"Your protector against what?" she asked, and I told her of how it was only just to protect myself and my jewel against people. And then I told her too of what it was most people would do if they knew it was there, because of how they were. Most of them.

Her look came back for some then, but after not so long she changed to being in her joking and good way again, quite soon. And she began then by asking if she could see it any.

"Could I?" she said. "Please?"

And just to stop us from having to argue anymore, I said "Okay." And I told her to look away some while I pulled my shirt up above it and unfastened the straps at my back.

"Are you ready yet?" she kept on by asking, and when I had pushed my shirt back in and put my protector on the table I said she could. And as soon as she saw my protector lying there she reached out and pulled it across the table towards her, by one of its straps.

She sat it down on her leg at first, so that it curved around like it curves around my stomach, and balanced there. And she studied the cuts at each corner where the straps go through, and laced one strap through its buckle to fasten it up, then she undid it again.

When she turned the protector around she began to laugh although, at all the pictures and the words that are still there on the other side from when it used to be a tray.

" 'A bird in the hand is worth two in the bush,' " she read out in a pretend voice, like as if she was teaching wisdom. Then, " 'Never put off until tomorrow what you can do today.' What other ones were on here, that you cut off?"

But I told her I couldn't remember, and instead she started pointing out the pictures and I went to stand behind her to see, and we laughed together.

"So what did it used to be, in the beginning?" Marie asked, and when I told her she asked me how long ago I'd made it.

"From just after Nalda went away," I said, and then she asked did I wear it all the time.

"Do you even sleep with it on?" she asked and did a smile, and I nodded. "So this is the first time you've been around anyone since then without having it on?"

And when I nodded again she made a funny laugh in a pretend voice, and made an evil face—like as if to pretend she had caught me out and she was just about to steal my jewel.

I was pleased that our arguing had stopped then, even although I knew she was only doing for a joke about my jewel. And even although I knew how very well she thought it wasn't there, I didn't mind so much now that we had stopped arguing. But guess what she asked me then, Marie, right after. She asked me why—considering I'd run off from so many places so many times, after only letting tiny bits slip—she asked me why it was I still hadn't run off from there, considering everything she knew. And I got stuck.

I didn't dare for a moment to say that it was only because of how I liked her so much that I had risked to stay, or any like that. So after saying nothing for too long, all I did say about was how I had got so tired of always running away from places, and not knowing anyone or things, and not being able to be like people are, that I'd decided I no longer cared if anyone robbed me or not. And I said of how I'd sometimes even almost longed for it, just to make it all be over. That last bit was the wrong thing although, because when I sneaked a look to Marie her face was getting so upset that I had to add, "But mostly it's only because I don't think you would tell to anyone. Because of how I trust you more . . ."

And then I quickly got lucky, cause I managed to think of a new thing completely, because of how I'd just looked at my clock.

"We've missed Frank and Elizabeth," I cried out, and Marie looked to her watch.

"So we have," she said. "I didn't know it was that late."

And slowly then, but still holding my protector in her hand, she got out from the spare chair and said of how it was time for her to go.

"I dare say you've had enough of me trying to convince you for one day anyway," she said.

And that was true, even although I would have still liked her to stay on some more. But I didn't say about either thing, I only just followed her to the door, and did my best to make a laugh when she said that she would continue with her mission tomorrow.

"Unless," she said, "unless, of course, I can feel anything now that you've got this thing off." And she pointed a finger out to start doing some more prodding again.

It hit off against one of my shirt buttons to begin with, and with her eyes closed—pretending to be all in excitement—Marie said, "I think I can feel something, Mr. Reynard. I think I can."

And then she opened her eyes to do a smile at me. When she did another prod after that although, my stomach did the strangest thing. It kind of jumped back and away from her finger all by its own, and even I was surprised by it.

"Heavens," Marie said. "You're almost like a sea-creature whose shell has been removed without this thing on." And she didn't prod anymore after that, she just looked to my face. And I looked to hers too, and stood still—and I could feel a kind of special thing.

"I suppose I'd better get going," Marie said, but we still kept on by just looking like that for some more, and just standing.

Then, at last, she gave my protector back to me, and I stood to wave and to watch her climb the lawns. And when she had gone, before I put my protector back on again, I lifted my shirt some and prodded around my stomach with my own finger.

But I couldn't make it do that jumping thing any, not by myself.

23

The next day, one of the very first things I did—after I had done a little bit of time in the garden—was to go looking for Elizabeth or Frank, just to say of how I was sorry for not coming up to their little room.

It was Frank I found first, inside the little room in fact. He was sitting drinking from a cup and reading a newspaper, and when I pushed the door open and came inside he looked to me over the top of his newspaper, and he did a big smile when he saw it was me.

"A good morning to you, Mr. Reynard," he said, folding his newspaper into half and then laying it down flat on his legs. And I did a smile back to him.

"It's just to say of how I'm sorry for not helping you last night," I said, "but I had to do a thing."

He didn't mind much although. He said of how he'd picked some himself instead, and he told me not to worry about it. But then he did a very strange kind of wink to me after that, and he said he understood perfectly. And just while I was feeling confused by that, the door opened and Elizabeth came into the room too.

"Oh, hello," she said. "This is a nice surprise."

"He just came up to apologise for bombing out on us last night," Frank said, and Elizabeth laughed. Then she touched the side of her nose with one finger and said that there was no need to worry about that—they understood fine. And all at once I had the feeling that they knew the real reason for why I hadn't been there, and that they knew all about of what I'd been doing instead. But I tried my very best not to let them see that. All I did was just say I'd better get back down to my work in the garden instead, and that I would see them both later, when it was the evening time. And then I left very carefully.

I got quite afraid when I was going down the lawns although, because I knew the only way they could know was if Marie had told them. And even although I wasn't afraid of Frank or Elizabeth doing anything to me, I wondered if it didn't mean that Marie would have told a whole lot of other people too, or even if Frank or Elizabeth might not tell someone else even. And I got very angry at myself for ever having told any of it in the first place, and when Marie came down to the gardens to see me in the afternoon, I got very angry with her too. And this is how it went, that time.

When she came at first I just went on by working, and didn't answer any of the things she said to me at all. And then when she asked me why I wasn't speaking any, and why I was making her be so unhappy again, I just said straight out that it was because of how she'd said all about my jewel to Elizabeth and Frank. And straight afterwards I said that probably she had done it to make them laugh and that she had probably told them it wasn't really there, like she believed. And all the time, when I looked up, she just stood silently—looking as if she was shocked by it all. And at first I thought she was pretending that way, just to make me think she didn't even know what I was talking about, so's I would believe she hadn't told them at all. But after a while, and after a few things she said, I got to thinking that maybe that was the truth. And maybe I really had shocked her, with all of my things I said.

"What on earth has made you think all this?" she asked me eventually, in a voice like she was surprised and also quite angry at the same time. "What makes you think I would do a thing like that?"

And because I was still thinking she was only pretending at that part, I said I hadn't thought she would do a thing like that, but that I knew she had. And I even said, imagine, that Frank and Elizabeth had told me so.

"Well what did they say?" she asked, becoming to be all distraught by then.

"They said you did," I told her.

"But I wouldn't do that . . ." she said.

And because there was a kind of pleading in her voice, I thought still that she was trying to cover up, and fool me more, and in an angry kind I said, "Yes you would."

Her face got to being angrier then, and her voice grew louder. And she said, "No I would not. And I'll even tell you why I wouldn't. I wouldn't do it because if anyone else besides me knew what you believe, they would think you were mad. They would, Mr. Reynard. And I don't want anyone to think that; not yet anyway. So tell me exactly what Frank and what Elizabeth said."

It made me very upset, all of when she said that. But it also made me see that she wasn't pretending any, so I told her exactly all of what had happened up in the little room. And, when I had done, she filled her cheeks with air and blew out loudly. And she let her arms fall loosely.

"Oh, you silly . . ." she said. "Silly . . ."

And what she said was, while she began to do a blush, she said it was obvious Frank and Elizabeth had thought we hadn't come to the little room at night because we'd become all romantic, with kissing and the such like. And I even blushed some too when she said it, and I asked her did she really think so, and she nodded.

"I honestly haven't told anyone," she said. "Truly."

So I said of how I was sorry, for telling about all those lies.

And then I became in a mood because of how she'd said I was mad.

Marie didn't get to know about my new mood although, not then, because almost as soon as we had finished by speaking about those things

131

she realised of how she was already late for getting back to work. And after a few more moments, she hurried off up the lawns again.

She asked me, before she left, if things were fixed out with us now, and if I wasn't angry at her anymore. And because of how wrong I'd been about Elizabeth and Frank, and because of how friendly Marie was trying to be, I said I wasn't, and that things were fixed out. But after she was gone, I kept on and on by thinking of what she'd said about how other people would think I was mad, and I let it grow.

It made me think on how that must be the thing she really thought about me. And that she kind of considered it her job to cure me of believing about my jewel before anyone else found out what I thought to be true. And it made me wish more and more that it would just come now, my jewel. And I even got a bit angry at it too, for not coming.

But the main thing was, I began remembering then about Marie's face when she'd told me the reason why Frank and Elizabeth thought we hadn't come up the night before. And the more I remembered it and thought on it, the more I was sure I could remember a thing in her expression which showed how silly, and how distasteful, that idea seemed to her. To me, it made me feel good, because of how much I would have liked for it to be the true thing. But I could tell from the way it embarrassed Marie that she only found it to be stupid.

And I even thought, right then, that she had probably gone straight off to correct Frank and Elizabeth as soon as she left. And although I was sure she wouldn't tell them the real reason for why we hadn't come up anymore, I was also sure she wouldn't want them to think she could possibly like me in the way I liked her.

The special way I hoped she didn't quite know about.

24

Two good things happened in that same afternoon although, which made my bad kind of mood mostly go away. The first thing was I bumped into Frank again, while I was up working at the walls of the hospital building. He was only just rushing past, and he didn't have any spare time to stop and talk to me with. But what he did do, he made exactly the same wink he'd made on me earlier in the day, and just before he disappeared around the corner he called out, "Someone's still looking very pleased with himself . . ."

And that made me know Marie hadn't rushed off first thing to put him straight, out of being so ashamed.

So that was the first thing, and the second was one that Marie did. She came out again later, while I was still working up at the building— tying those climbing things that had grown some onto higher parts of their supports. And what she did, she said how would I like it if, later on, instead of me cooking food for us both again, how would I like it if she gave me a rest and took me out to a special place for eating that she knew about, and bought food for us both there.

I was kind of nervous to think about it at first, but she said I would enjoy it a lot, and that I could have just whatever thing I wanted to eat. So in the end I said I would go, and once she had gone back to work it made me feel very happy to think about it, and not hardly nervous at all.

She'd said she would finish up with working a little bit earlier than usual again, and I was to be ready. And then we would go. So just as soon as I was finished with working on all of those climbing things I tidied my tools away for the day and went down to my little quarters to get cleaned up.

I didn't have any kinds of special clothes that I could wear or anything, just all of my usual tatty ones. But I put on some clean kinds of those and then, after that, I went back up to the hospital building again, to sit outside on the bench where all of the patients and old Will come to each day.

I tried to work out, while I was sitting there waiting, why Marie had decided to take me to that place. And I worked out, too, that it was probably only because there would be other people there, and around. Which meant it would be too dangerous and risky for me to say all things about my jewel, and then she wouldn't have to listen to it anymore. Probably, I thought, she only just wanted to have a rest from arguing about that always. But it didn't make me sad or angry to think of that, not on this time. And when I had worked it out I just watched quietly over the garden, at how nice it was in the last bits of the sun, and I waited for her to come out.

It turned out that the place Marie knew about wasn't all that far from the shops where I always go to, to buy my food and things from. And sometimes—when I was passing it some days—I had even looked at it, and looked in through the windows at all the people eating there inside.

And the thing was too, whenever I'd looked in there at the people like that, I'd always had this feeling like about how good it would be to be able to be a person like that, and to be in there. All with friends and with families and things. So when we got close to the place, and Marie pointed out that that was where we were going to, I grew more excited than ever inside, and all the rest of my bad kind of mood went away completely.

I asked Marie if she didn't think my clothes were too tatty for to be allowed inside of there although, and I looked to spy at them in a shop window we passed. She said they were fine, but they still looked quite

134

tatty to me. Especially if they were to be compared with hers. She had changed from her nurse's clothes to having a white shirt with arms much wider than her own arms, and a kind of man's waistcoat on top of that. And she had untied her loops too, and put on a necklace chain, and I really was only tatty compared. I looked at my crazy fox hair and my beard in the window secretly too, and even they were tatty. If you had seen us both you would never have thought, not ever, that I was the one with the special thing inside. No one would have.

But all of that made me feel even more amazed once we got inside the restaurant; to be there where people go, looking so tatty as I was. And to be there with Marie too, looking so beautiful as she was. It was very unlikely and strange for me, and because it was so precious I began to do that thing of hanging onto the minutes again.

There was a man inside the restaurant who showed us what table we could have, and when we got there he pulled back a chair for Marie to sit in, and then he pulled one back for me too. And all he said to me was, "Sir."

Just that. And that was only the second time anyone had ever once called me that name.

Marie did a smile to me once I had sat down some, probably because she could see how strange I thought things were. And then, when the man gave us both a book each, all I did was say thank you to him, because I didn't know of what it was. And I only just put it down on my table without even opening it up, and Marie laughed then.

It turned out that what it was, the book told you inside what you could have, to eat. And what you could choose from. And when I had learned about it all I chose a kind of chicken, because of how I thought that would be a joke for Marie.

After that the man took our books back from us and he went off, to make the food we had chosen I think. And it took him quite a while to do that.

135

"So," Marie said to me when he had gone away, "are there no things left that you're angry with me about tonight?"

And somehow, because I wasn't thinking so much, and even because I was only just so happy, I said straight out, "Only one thing." And then I wished for it to be that I hadn't said it.

"Well what's that?" Marie asked me in a kind of surprise, and I decided that all I could do by then was to tell. So I dropped my voice away down into a whisper, to make sure as no one else around would hear. And then I said, "You think I'm mad, to believe that I have a . . . special thing, inside."

And Marie shook her head.

"I believe you do have a special thing inside," she whispered back. And for that tiny second again, I thought that at last she'd come to believe it. But then she said, "And I believe that Nalda believed it too. But it's not a diamond, Mr. Reynard."

And I could see things were just the same, so I asked a new question about the restaurant, so's I could get back to how it felt to be there, with Marie, and not grow all unhappy again.

I asked about things like that right up until the man had finished with making our food for us and brought it out to our table. I asked about this water with creatures inside, which Marie said was for people to choose from for their dinner, if what they wanted to eat was one of those creatures. And I asked too about these sticks on the table, and Marie said they were to take out any pieces of food that got stuck inside the spaces between your teeth.

When we had begun to eat our food although, and the man had gone away again—after spreading out a square cloth on each of our knees for us—Marie said a special thing which made me excited enough to be able to stop saying about all those other questions, and I'll tell you about what it was.

I was just trying to pull a piece of my chicken away from its bone, and Marie was drinking some from her glass with wine inside, and then she

136

put her glass down and leaned a bit closer to me across the table, and she began to speak.

"I've had this really good idea I'd like to tell you about," she said, while she pushed some stray loops back behind her ear. "It came to me this afternoon, in the hospital, while I was thinking about your jewel."

I jumped a bit at that although, and I looked quickly about—to see if anyone else had heard. I knew Marie didn't think it was dangerous to be talking out loud like that, because of how she didn't believe about any of it being true anyway. But I asked her to keep her voice a bit more quiet after that, because of how it was dangerous.

"Sorry," she said. "Sorry. But listen, I've thought of a way we can find out for sure or not." Then she did a smile and said that it didn't even include having to cut me open. "Up in the hospital," she told, "there's a machine that takes pictures of people's insides. Of their bones, and to find out what's in their stomachs and things. It's up on the third floor."

And that was the thing that made me so excited, because I knew that if we could use it then I could prove everything to her for once and for all. And straight away I asked her if we'd be able to use it.

"We could with a bit of planning," she said, and my excitement grew to be even more. And as we ate the rest of our food I asked her all kinds of things about how it worked, and what it did.

It was called an X-ray machine, Marie said, but most of it, really, I didn't understand so much. I did understand that the machine would be able to make a photograph of the inside of my stomach although. And when Marie printed the photograph it would show my diamond right inside there, like a bright white dot on the black picture.

It didn't even make me much unhappy to think that Marie had only thought of it to prove to me there was no jewel there. I knew that was the reason for why, but it only meant she would very soon find out the opposite to be true. And none of the other things she said after that made me angry or sad in the same way they usually would have done.

•

We both had this kind of a cake after our main food, which you had to eat with a fork instead of a spoon, and which tasted very special. And after that Marie called out to the man who had made it all and asked for the piece of paper that told how much we had to pay.

I spied on that and it had a very expensive price written on, much more than I would ever have been able to pay, but Marie didn't seem to mind by any. And while she took it up to the counter I brought one of the tooth picks from the table, and went to watch the creatures in the water tank for a while. Then, when Marie had finished paying, she came across to get me and we left.

25

Shall we go up to see Frank and Elizabeth when we get back?"
Marie asked on our way along the road, and I said "Yes." "I
suppose it'll save them talking about us, at least," she said, and I
watched to see her doing a blush again.

I picked inside the spaces of my teeth with my stick while we walked,
even although there was really no food in between. And now and again
Marie pretended to be trying to take it from me, and said to stop doing
it some. "That's really not good etiquette, Mr. Reynard," she said, in a
pretend voice of someone very old and rich. "What will the Winslows
think if they should see us? It really is too disgusting for words."

But I was very happy. I was very happy all along that way back to the
hospital, especially with the things I was thinking.

I thought of how good it was to be outside with Marie, almost like a
friend. And I thought too of how many unhappy times I'd had walking
along that way on my own in the past; times when I'd been unhappy
about having still to wait for my jewel, and work in the garden; and
times when I'd been unhappy about not being able to be just like people are, people I passed and people I could see all around.

Walking there then it made me even happier to think over all of that,
somehow, and especially to think how unlikely it would have seemed to
me on one of those times if I was to think I would ever be doing this;
walking along there with Marie, almost like her friend. And, especially,
having just been with her to that place, which I could never have imagined myself in. Not while my jewel was still to come, at least.

What made me happiest of all although, was to think upon how Marie would soon become even more of my friend, and that nights like this

would happen again and again and again. Because soon she'd know the things I'd said were true, and she'd have to believe them.

"Will it only be both of us who see my photograph although?" I asked Marie, when we were almost back by the hospital. Because of how I didn't want anyone else knowing all about my secret.

"I think I should be able to work that out," Marie said. "Someone else might have to help us take the photograph, but I know all about the developing machine. So we can make sure no one else is around when we do that."

I asked her too, as we were going through the hospital corridors towards the little room, just how soon we would be able to do it. And she said that, if things worked out right, there was a good chance we would be able to do it the very next night. And so, by the time we got to the room to see Elizabeth and Frank, I was just about as happy as I could ever be.

Frank already had his horse lists out when we went in through the door. He was sitting with them spread out on the table, studying them carefully. And Elizabeth was sitting with her feet up on a chair in front, looking quietly at the TV and holding a glass with port in her hand. They only stayed like that for a tiny second after we had opened the door although, and then they both looked up at the same time, and they both grinned and began to speak at the same time too.

"Here they are," Frank said, while Elizabeth lifted her glass up higher and said "Hello" to us both. Then she put her feet down onto the floor and put her glass beside Frank's lists on the table.

"Come on in properly and sit down," she said, and she got up to get us both a drink. "Come on," she said. "Settle down and then tell us all about what you've been up to."

And I heard Frank make a little laugh at that.

"Nothing too graphic though," he said quietly. "Spare us old folks our modesty."

I took the chair next to his then, and Marie sat in the seat Elizabeth had been resting her feet on.

"We've been out having dinner on Stanton Road," Marie said, and Elizabeth made a sound that sounded impressed.

"That must have cost you," Frank said. "I think we must be paying you too much, Mr. Reynard."

When Marie said of how it was her who paid although, Frank put his hand upon my back some, and said, "A kept man, eh? Good for you," and he laughed loudly.

Marie said some stuff about what it had been like then, and while she was doing that, and while Elizabeth was asking her all about what we'd had, I stopped picking at my teeth with my stick for a short time. And, instead, I used it to pick out my long odds horses from the list. I closed my eyes and put it down amongst all the possible horses, and when I opened my eyes I just wrote down the name of the one it was pointing at. And then I did the same thing again.

Frank didn't notice me the first time I don't think, but he did see what I did the second time, and I knew because I heard him laughing before I'd even opened my eyes back up. And when I was writing down the horse's name he said, "Good enough, Mr. Reynard. Good enough. And if you get as lucky with horses as you seem to have gotten with the ladies then we'll do just fine."

I blushed some at that, and I wrote the name of the horse down as slowly as I could, just so's as I could keep my head down and hidden for as long as possible.

Luckily for me, although, Elizabeth asked me how I had enjoyed the restaurant and my meal, just as I finished off putting down the very last letter of the horse, and that helped me out. I got quite excited too, telling about it all. Telling about the man who made the food, and his books, and the cloths he put on our knees. And telling too about how it was to be in there with all such people, and how I'd often been in places on my own to eat before, but how it was always just a kind of noisy or a very quiet place where you chose your own food and then took it off to a seat, and no one ever came anywhere near you.

I got going so much that I almost even said some stuff about how special it was to be there with Marie, and how good it had been walking home. And I believe, if I hadn't been watching myself, I would have told all about the photograph I was going to have taken too. But I stopped myself from all of that just in time, and instead I went on about the creatures in the water for a while.

By the time I finished up I felt quite tired, and everyone was smiling. Which I suppose was just because of how stupid and long and boring they thought I was. But I didn't even mind that so much. I was still happy. And after I was finished we still had a good time, playing some games of cards. And while we played I had a feeling of how good it was that I had come to know Frank and Elizabeth so well, added to Marie. I even tried to work out how long I'd been working at the hospital, how long it was since I'd ran from my last place, because I knew it hadn't been so very long. But if I thought back to how alone I'd always been then, and compared it to how joined in I was here, it was a difference that I thought would have taken a hundred years to make. Or at least to make so strong.

It came to be my turn at cards while I was thinking through all that stuff although, and everyone called my name out because of how I was lost so far off, and wasn't paying attention. They even teased me some about having been in such a dream, while I was sorting out the cards in my hand. And when I put down the one I'd chosen, and they all went quiet again to concentrate on the game, I had just about the strangest idea from ever. I began to think of just about the strangest thing.

It was mostly because of how good it was to be amongst such things there, and because of how happy it made me to be like that. And what I began to think, I began to dream of what if everything Marie had been saying to me was true. Of what if, when she took that picture, it showed my stomach really just empty inside—with nothing else in there. And I began to dream too of how that would mean I was just exactly like a real and normal person, with no longer any need to be afraid, and no need to ever once run away again. And although it would mean I wouldn't never get to have all the rich and luxurious things I'd always thought about, I wouldn't even mind so much. Because, instead, I could always just stay at the hospital forever then, and even though I'd have to always garden I could also come up to visit with Elizabeth and Frank every evening, and even make some more new friends, because of how I would have no need to be afraid.

And, most of all, I would get to make full and proper friends with Marie.

It was a very strange thing for me to be thinking, I knew. But all while we played with the cards I kept on by doing it, and even started by hoping that maybe my photograph wouldn't find anything there, no jewel at all.

And so, when Frank and Elizabeth had gone home for the night, and Marie asked me if I wasn't just a little bit nervous about the next day, I only shook my head and said I wasn't. Not any.

"But what if it should turn out there is no jewel there, Mr. Reynard?" she said. "I know you don't think that's possible, but . . . just imagine, for me, that it did turn out that way. How would that make you be?"

And I did a smile to her and only said it would make me be happy, because it would mean I was free from the danger. And she did a smile back to me then.

"You know," she said, "I think we're going to be alright, Mr. Reynard. I really do." And she went to pour some port for us both. And to flip around with the channels on the TV.

She said quite a strange thing just some times after that although. A thing that I didn't really understand. It was while I was watching the screen, and listening to some of the things the people on there were saying. And just when one of them did say a thing I heard Marie make a tutting sound, and then she began to talk on, right over the top of what they were saying.

143

"You know," she said, "in a way you're a lot luckier than most people, Mr. Reynard. It's just unfortunate that more people can't see that what they believe to be the truth, and that what they build their lives around . . . It's just a shame there's not a camera to point it all out for them so easily."

She even seemed to get quite excited then, and instead of just looking at the screen like she had been doing till then she turned around to look at me instead.

"Just think of all the people who were sitting around us in the restaurant tonight," she said. "Just imagine all of the things they've been taught about themselves, or about the world, that they just take as being true, when they really might not be. And maybe it's something they think is keeping them up when really it's keeping them down. Or maybe it's something they think will lead them into the world when really it's what's keeping them out. But there's no camera that will ever let them see it that way, and then force them to rearrange. And they just walk forever away."

I think she must have known how confused I was just from my face although, because she soon laughed and apologised, and told me not to mind about it any—not tonight at least. Then she picked up the cards that were still there on the table, and said to let her say a joke she had thought about when Frank and Elizabeth were still there instead.

"Alright," I said, and she looked through the pack, forwards and back and forwards again, until she pulled out this one card that was the one she wanted.

"I thought I'd better not say anything while they were still here playing," she said. "But look, this one here is you. The king of diamonds." And she held it up close to a light and said she was trying to see through its stomach, to see if there was any kind of a diamond inside.

I said it couldn't be me although, because of how it had both halves of its face on the same side, and because of how I don't.

"Imagine if you did though," Marie said. "That would really be something."

144

And then I began to pretend to her of how I had seen someone just like that in the restaurant, over near the tank the creatures were in. But she didn't believe me although. She said it wasn't true. But still, I kept on by pretending to her for a while about it anyway. Just for fun.

We left quite soon after that, Marie and me. I rinsed water in our glasses while she was unplugging the TV and putting away the cards. And when she wasn't looking I put our glasses very close to each other at the sink, so that they were even touching. And then we turned out the lights, and from outside I locked up the door.

The best thing from any time ever happened when we passed out through the main door into the night although. I pushed the door open and went out first, and when Marie came out behind me she said, "You are very brave, Mr. Reynard. There aren't many people who would let that photograph be taken, even if it could be done."

And then she reached forward . . . and she kissed me. She kissed me just one time on the lips. And while I stood there all in a shock she said she would come down to the garden in the morning, to let me know what time she could sneak me into that place.

And then she was gone.

I lay awake for a while on my bed after I had undressed, really just amazed. And kind of overjoyed, to think that Marie had kissed me. I got so excited, in fact, with thinking about that, and with thinking about my photograph too, that I couldn't even get myself to go to sleep. And I just lay there for a long time, tapping my fingers on my protector, and turning all kinds of all things over.

I thought about how amazed I would have been, on the days when Maude used to come down, to know that once, in the same special day, I would get to eat in that place with Marie, and be kissed by her also. And then I thought too about how I'd sometimes very much hated the garden, and longed for my jewel to come just so's I could be long gone.

Eventually, although, once I'd begun to long for sleep and it still wouldn't come, I began to try and think more about having that picture taken, and I tried to decide of whether I most wanted the jewel to be there, or to not be there. I still knew it was there really, and I could even feel it moving around a tiny amount. But although I was looking forward to seeing Marie's face all in surprise when she made up the picture, I did still wish a little bit that, by some kind of magic, it could turn out that my stomach was only empty. And I saw this picture of me just like a proper man, and instead of all my gardening clothes I was wearing this suit, standing at a railway place talking to all these other people. And then I saw this other one of me wearing a pair of sports shoes, and playing all these games. But I suppose, really, that must have been me beginning to drift in and out of sleep, because that's just about all I can remember of, until I woke up this morning, and began to grow excited again.

26

Marie came smiling down the lawns this morning almost as soon as I had begun working, all bright in the sun. And the moment she reached down to where I was she said, "Around five this evening. Everything's set."

And I only had time to look up and do a smile before she hurried off back up to the hospital buildings, with her loops falling around on her shoulders.

I grew to be more excited than I had ever been before although, from then on into the day. I got so excited that I even did most of my work quite badly, just because of how I couldn't concentrate properly. And each time I did something wrong I just thought of how I would put it right tomorrow, and not worry any today. And I continued to look forward to it being five o'clock.

But halfway through the day, when old Will and the rest came out onto the benches, it seemed almost as if time had stopped, and I thought the evening might never get around to coming. Everything just seemed to be going so slow, and I even got to worrying that something would go wrong before five o'clock came. That Marie would come down to say we could no longer use the machine. Or even that someone who had overheard us saying a thing in the restaurant would come to stalk me out, and that would be an end to it. For a while I even kept turning around quickly, or looking over on my shoulder, almost expecting someone to be there. But no one ever was, and I slowly forgot about that. And slowly the time did move, and four o'clock came, and then a half past of it. And when it got to being just ten minutes before five o'clock Marie appeared by my side again, and without either of us speaking she helped me to put all my tools away in the sheds, and then we climbed the lawns together.

"How are you feeling?" she asked me, just as we were crossing the path to the hospital doors, and I told her I was feeling good. I was really feeling a bit nervous in my stomach by then, but I didn't tell her about that any, just in case it meant we couldn't use the machine on me, or something.

"Alright," Marie said, opening the doors. "It's up on the third floor, so we'll take the lifts."

I had never been anywhere but the bottom floor before, so I had to follow Marie all the way. We walked out into a main corridor when we came out of the lifts, and then through all kinds of twists and turns, sometimes seeing a sign which said "X-Ray" pointing in the way we were going.

We eventually got there too, and Marie pushed this door open, and held it for me to go in through first, into a room which looked very strange.

There was a huge machine right in the middle of the room, with a table to lie on, and then all these other things above it. And over in the corner of the room was something with a little window on it, and everything else hidden behind.

"Well, this is us . . ." Marie said, as she walked over to the big machine, and she hit her hand on the side of it.

"I'll explain to you exactly how everything works first," she said. "To stop you from feeling afraid of anything. And then we'll get started."

So, to begin with, she pointed to the big part which hung above the table I was to lie on, and she said that was really just a big light.

"We move it down to the part of you we want to photograph," she said, "then we put the film beneath you, fire the light, and it'll go right through your body onto the film. Only," she said, and held one single finger up, "it won't be able to go through anything solid, like your bones. Or your diamond. So all of those things will leave a mark on the film."

We went across to the little place with the window after that, and Marie said the person taking the picture made the camera work from there.

"These controls set how long the light stays on for, and how bright it is. Stuff like that. And this one here fires it to take the photograph. That's about all there is to it really. Does it make any kind of sense to you yet?"

And when I said it did we went back to the main machine, to get started.

First of all, what Marie did was lift up a lid on the table part, and she put this square box inside which she said was the film. Then, after that, it was time for me to get up and lie out on the table. So that's what I did.

"Lift your shirt up now," Marie said to me, and when I did that she laughed. "I'd forgotten all about that," she said, and she rapped her nails on my protector. "You'll have to take that off too." So I sat up again to unfasten it, and when it was undone Marie put it inside a cupboard and I lay back down.

"Okay," she said. "You just wait there, and I'll go and get Francis to come and set the times. I won't be long. And Francis won't get to see the photograph, so don't worry about a thing."

Then, just before she left, she touched my stomach lightly with a finger, and she laughed when it jumped.

"Still exactly like a shellfish," she said, and she went outside.

I was feeling fine at first there, still all in excitement, and looking forward to the photograph being taken. But Marie stayed away for a very long time, and while I was lying there like that my stomach got to be quite cold. And the longer Marie stayed away the more nervous I became, and I kept on by wishing she would just hurry up.

Then, suddenly, after a bit more time, I found myself gripped by this terrible fear. It was when I felt myself almost falling asleep some, and I wondered why I was so tired. And all at once I became certain that something wasn't right. I had been lying there far too long, and right then I got to having the idea that none of this had anything to do with a camera. None at all. What had happened, I slowly worked out, was Marie had believed in my jewel all along, and she had only done all of that arguing for so long to keep me from knowing, while she made a plan with a few other people. And now, I thought, I was just about to have an operation to have it removed, to have it stolen.

I leapt up from the table then. I jumped down onto the floor, only stopping to take my protector out from its cupboard, and then I rushed out of the room and ran just as fast as I could.

I had no idea how to get out from there really, but I just kept on by following these signs which said "Fire Exit" until I came to a door which I had to push a bar to open. I think too, when I did, that it made this alarm go off, but I hardly even thought about that at the time. I just ran down the steps as fast as I could, two and three at a time, holding onto my protector by one of its straps and hoping each turn in the stairs would be the last.

I had to pass through one more of those doors with the bars on, but once I did that I was outside, at the front of the hospital, not the back where the gardens are. I could hear that alarm ringing more properly by then, and I could hear lots and lots of people shouting too. I even thought I might have heard someone shouting, "Mr. Reynard." But I don't know for sure, and I didn't turn around to look. I just kept on by running and running. Running faster and faster and as fast as I could, until I saw I was near to the train station. Then I ran to there, ran through, and got onto a train which was just leaving. And I stayed on that all night until it brought me to this place where I am still now. Waiting in yet another hotel room for my shaking to subside.

●

I spent a long time thinking on that train tonight about how I could possibly have gotten Marie so wrong, how I could never once have suspected her before. The thing even is, too, that just a few days ago I'd decided I was going to spend my emergency money on buying her a special present, like a bracelet I'd saw, or maybe a special picture, just because of how I thought I wouldn't never need to use it again. But that's one stroke of luck I suppose, that I hadn't done that yet, or else I could have been in some real trouble tonight. And I wouldn't have been able to stay in this room at all.

It's mostly just like all the others I've had, this place, like you would know. But, to be true, I've cried a lot more in it than I ever did before. I've had much more tears. Just to think, I suppose, of how different things will be from how they've been for the last while.

On all the other times when I ran it didn't make much difference to me really. All it was, was just starting the same thing again in a different place, and nothing much was to be changed. But on this time the thought of going back to such a lonely way—with no friends—it's almost more than I can bear. And I've been cursing myself inside sometimes that I wasn't brave enough to just stay there by lying on that table, and let them take whatever they wanted to take from me, to get an end to it all.

It must be the true thing, you see, that some people really can tell that I have a special thing inside. Just by looking. That's what I've worked out from all my thinking tonight. And what I've decided is, I think they probably can't tell what my special thing is, but only that I have one. And I think that's only what Marie could tell to begin with. Probably from that very first time when she studied me properly up at the benches with Elizabeth. And then she probably got Elizabeth and Frank to help her out, and that's for why Frank was probably always going on about his faith, and why he asked me if I had a thing of my own too that time, just so's as Marie could be sure she wasn't wasting her time. And then she probably kept telling me about how untrue all of Nalda's things were just so's as she could keep on by getting to know more and more, and so's she could also get my special trust, while she made her whole plan.

And, probably, she even put a special kind of a spell onto me too. To get me to feeling all of that way about her.

151

It still gets me to weeping some although when I think of how I felt just last night, and I think of how it made me feel when I wished that we might find my jewel not to be there, just so's I could turn out to be a normal kind, and stay forever to be friends with Elizabeth and Frank and Marie in the garden. But I suppose Nalda was right about all people, and how they would do just about anything to make some gain. And even pretend to be your friend in that way.

So always, from now, it must be that I hide myself most more than ever. To keep anyone from seeing whatever it is that gives me away. And I'll only just find a garden where there's no one to be there but me, and break my back while I wait.

All until my jewel will come, and make me free.